D1606146

Treacherous

Special thanks to the art designer on the cover,
Rosa Risque.

This for the savages, this for the savages
This shit Treacherous - Lil Durk

Prologue

Walking home from school was the worst today. It was over 100 degrees and the long sleeve uniform shirt only added to my already drenched underarms. I couldn't wait until I turned sixteen because my parents promised me a car.

"Urhhh." I turned to look over at Rihanna who was fuming. I could tell by the look on her face that Dray hadn't answered his phone still; normally he would give us a ride but today he basically left us standing out in the heat.

"It's okay, we almost home now, Ri Ri."

"I know but it's hot. This ain't like him to just leave us hanging."

"What if something's wrong?" I tried to justify it.

"Bullshit. That foo probably somewhere up in Jasmine's ass." She shook her head. I could tell she wanted to cry and all I could do was shake my head. Dray was a dog. He was so much of a dog he made me not want a boyfriend ever. Although I only focused on my education like my parents asked, I still didn't want a lying cheating dog. Plenty of guys tried to talk to me every time we stepped foot in the projects but I paid them no mind. Most called me stuck up but oh well, I wasn't one of them easy chicks that fell for thugs. I made a pact to myself that when I got older and did find a man he would be perfect. I didn't have time for the heartbreak that came with dating a street nigga.

"What's going on at your house?" Rihanna said, bringing me from my daze. I looked up and noticed an abundance of cop cars surrounding my home. My parents worked as agents but these cars belonged to the local police department. I steadied my pace and hurried towards my home. Just as I made it, the coroner's office was bringing a body out *covered in a white sheet. My heart fell into my gut not knowing who could be under the sheet. Shortly after, another gurney was being rolled out and on top there was another body covered.*

"Reina, oh my God." I heard Rihanna saying but I remained mute. Without warning, I ran across the yellow tape that clearly read **Do Not Cross.** *I could hear the officers yelling and scrambling, trying hard to get to me but that didn't stop me from running over to the bodies. I lifted the sheet and my father laid lifeless. There was a bullet hole etched in the front of his head with a slight bit of blood seeping from inside. Just as I collapsed, I could feel someone snatch me up.*

"She lives here!" I faintly heard Rihanna yell in the background. Tears began to pour from my eyes as I looked over to see them rolling the other body into the coroner's van. I was praying to myself that it wasn't my mother but something in my heart told me it was.

"Hello, Renia, I'm Mrs. Alexander. I worked with your mother and father. I know you're hurting right now but I need you to bear with me." She bent down and held her knees so she could come eye level with me on the ground. "Reina, I need you to shape up. If you don't talk to me, these people are gonna send you to foster care. Do you hear me?" she asked and hearing her say foster care alerted me. I nodded my head yes and gave her my undivided attention. "Do you have anybody you could call to come get you?" Again, I nodded my head yes. I vividly remember my mother saying, "if anything ever happened to us, call your uncle, Franko." Franko wasn't really my uncle but he was a good friend to both my mother and father. "Can you call them?"

"Yes." I wept as I pulled my iPhone from my backpack. Before I could dial Franko's number, I heard his voice lingering behind me. I looked in the direction and sure enough he was heading towards us.

"Reina, let's go sweetheart." He reached his hand out to me. I looked from his hand to his face and he wore the slightest bit of emotion. This was strange for a man that loved my parents dearly. They both were dead and his face was pale. I bit into my bottom lip and when I thought about the foster care I could be sent to I lifted from the ground. As Franko guided me towards the streets, I watched the van with my parents' bodies inside until it disappeared.

"Let's go, love." Franko brought me from what I was hoping was a

nightmare. I looked at him and we connected eyes. He quickly dropped his head and opened the passenger side door. I climbed in reluctantly and immediately peered out the window. As Franko started his engine, he pulled from alongside the curb. Rihanna and I locked eyes and I could see the empathy in her eyes. My heart was crying and I could tell she felt my pain. We held each other's gaze until the car pulled off, and for some strange reason I felt I would never see my friend again.

One

Queen

"So when will I see you again?" John asked with much frustration in his voice. His cheeks had turned a rosy red and I could tell he was tired of my comings and goings. Before he could say another word, I used my index finger to "shhh" him. I seductively placed a gentle kiss on his lips then forehead. Without another word, I quickly darted to the window I had previously come through, and just like that, I vanished into the night air. I didn't bother to look back at John who I could feel in the window pensively watching me. I knew he was tired of my shit but he was well satisfied so I left him without any explanation or remorse for his underlying love. What John and I had was a mere illusion. And it was just that.

The story with me and John was a crazy one but something had blossomed from it. John was a guy that I had followed for a few months on a hit. He turned out to be the wrong person but a sexual satisfaction kept me coming back. His blonde hair and blue eyes attracted me to him so I used my seductiveness to lay him. He was married with four children so it was nothing but sex. However, the lust in his eyes craved more of me than I could give him. With the demented life I lived, I made time to climb through his bedroom window and give him the satisfaction his wife couldn't. Because he started off as prey, I knew everything about him from his work schedule to his account number. I knew where his kids went to school and even where his wife got her hair done.

The first time I went through John's window, he was scared shitless. I used my nine millimeter to force him into a chair that sat on the opposite side of his bed. I duct-taped his mouth and tied his hands together behind him. I seductively walked around him and stood in front of him like the stallion I was. I bent down and whispered in his ear, "I won't bite," above a whisper, making him shiver in his seat. Once I had found out he wasn't my mark, I took advantage of him sexually. Using one hand to unbuckle his pants, I slid down his zipper and took his love tool into my hand. When I wrapped my lips around it, he melted. I slowly began to bop my head and suddenly his body relaxed. I sucked his medium-sized penis like it would give me life and I wasn't gonna stop until I proved my point. Because it had been so long since I got laid, I needed his fix like a starving addict. It had been years since I had a piece of meat in my life so boy oh boy I would take advantage of this moment. By the time I was done sucking the life out of John, he was well satisfied and I was satisfied I had left my mark. I vanished as quickly as I came without leaving a trace. After that night, I returned a few weeks later for another sexscapade, and after that, it has been a normal routine.

Ring...Ring...Ring...

My phone vibrated inside the pocket of my leather biker jacket. I silently cursed seeing that it was Franko calling.

"Hello."

"Hey, Renia. I need you at that location at 11:00pm sharp. He's moving out about 1:30am; call me if you need me, sweetie."

"I'm on it," I replied quickly to rush Franko off my phone.

"Chow."

"Chow." I hung up just as I was making my way into my condo. I looked at my grandfather clock that hung over the fireplace and noticed it was only 8:30pm. I had time to shower and relax a bit before going on my job. Tonight I had a hit on an Italian mob boss, who, for some reason the mayor wanted dead. When it came to my job, I never asked questions because it wasn't my business. My business was to show up, kill and collect my money. That's it, that's all. And this is what my boring ass life consisted of.

I was a well paid assassin. No husband, no kids and no family. I was born Renia "Queen" Clarke to King Darrell Clarke and Laura Valentina Clarke, my mother who decided to keep her last name. Both my parents who worked as CIA agents, which was how they had met, were killed when I was 14 years old. I had no other family. No aunts, no sisters and brothers, *no one*. That's how I ended up with Franko. He was my dad's good friend, and although he was a part of the life of crime, they loved that man dearly.

Franko took me in, and trained me to become an assassin at an early age. By the time I was 16 years old, I had 26 bodies under my belt and didn't see myself stopping anytime soon. The passion of killing had grown on me and not to mention I loved the money. Though I grew up with wealthy parents and I was used to the finer things, the enjoyment of having my own cash was sweet. My mother and father worked so much I fell victim to the streets; I even hustled a little to pass time. I would leave school and go hang out in the Long Island City projects just about everyday.

I had a teenage friend named Rihanna, whom I haven't seen in years but she was the one that kept me grounded. When my parents were murdered, everything in my life changed. I lost contact with my puppy love boyfriend who I knew one day I would give my goodies too. I was very young when me and Donald dated so I was still a virgin by the time I moved away. At the tender age of 22, I had finally lost my virginity to my first love, Marcellus. Three years into our relationship, Marcellus was gunned down in front of my eyes.

After his death, that was the last straw for me. I buried myself into a shell, even ignoring Franko. His death was all my fault and that shit haunted me until this day. Cellus didn't know what I did for a living so his blood was basically on my hands. No one knew but Franko and I, and I made sure to keep it that way. Cellus had been the only man I had ever been with until I started slipping into John's window. Every chance I got, I took flowers to Cellus's grave. I rarely visit my parents grave because I was always left distraught. It pained me each time I left their gravesites so I chose to stay away. I had so many great memories of my parents, so seeing a headstone with their portraits didn't do it for me.

Walking past the mirror in my condo, I stopped to admire myself in the full length mirror. I had my mother's Colombian descent, and because my father was black, my skin tone was like deep honey. Because I had to stay in shape, my body was pure perfection. My hair fell to the middle of my back and because of my hazel eyes and pointy nose, people said I favored a younger Stacey Dash. However, looks aren't what paid me; passion for murder is what got me by. Here I was today, the most treacherous woman to walk the streets and anything else was forbidden.

Two

Queen

Admiring the black silk dress that clung to my every curve, I looked damn good for someone that was on a mission to kill. The split up my thigh was sexy and the black garter belt around my thigh exhilarated my look. I decided to keep it simple with my diamond bracelet and one small diamond ring. I wore my thin gold rope that had a picture of my parents inside the locket because I never took it off. Grabbing my diamond clutch from the bed, I grabbed the keys to the black Aston Martin Franko had rented then left my condo for the night's event.

As I drove through the streets of New York, the city was lit with it being a Saturday night. The party was located on One Beacon Court which was about 25 miles from my home. The sounds of Mary J. Blige *Share My World* played softly through the speakers and the glare from the full moon shone through my front windshield. I fell into a daze that I referred to as the *daze of my life*. I often had these visions of playing in the sun with my children. Two children, a boy and a girl. A white picket fence surrounded us as a small puppy chased a ball. My husband would come through the gate holding Chinese food because he knew it was my favorite. I don't know why, but this was always the semblance of an illusion. In this line of work, I had to continually tell myself *love doesn't exist.* So all thoughts of a husband and family would quickly escape my mind.

As I swooped the rental into a spiral driveway I was met with the valet. Opening my door for me he pulled my hand to help me out. Smiling, I thanked him and headed for the stairs. The party was in full swing and the entire home was filled to capacity. I scanned the crowd in search of Acosta and my eyes fell onto him across the room. Looking around, I watched the guard that stood at the top of the balcony and two who were nearby Acosta's side. I looked down at my watch and it was 12:26, which gave me an hour to make my move.

"Oh, honey, you look fabulous."

I turned around to the Caucasian woman that had complimented me.

"Thank you." I smiled.

As the waitress walked by, I grabbed a flute of wine and drank the entire glass in one swallow. I then headed for the bar so I could begin my job.

"Excuse me, do you have Dom Perignon?"

"Yes, would you like a glass or a bottle?"

"I'll take a bottle."

"Okay, that will be $1900." The bartender headed over to retrieve the bottle. When he came back, I handed him the credit card with an alias name Rebecca White.

"Can you give me two glasses?"

"Sure." He placed the glasses on the countertop and handed me back the card. I opened the bottle of champagne and began pouring a glass. I quickly dropped the pill into the glass and when I turned around...

"You have expensive taste," a masculine voice spoke enticingly.

When my eyes landed on him, I was taken aback. He was the most handsome creature that possibly walked this earth. He was nice and tall with the body of an athlete. The two-piece suit he wore didn't do him any justice at hiding how fit he was. He bit into his bottom lip and oh my God his lips were to die for. He had piercing eyes that were dark with the perfect oval shape. His locks were neatly twisted and he had them pulled back at the top and the back hung a little past his shoulders. The huge rocks in his ears let me know he was hood and I didn't have to ask what he was doing here. Drug dealer. Acosta was a mob boss that pushed weight all over the state. Hell, scratch that, he pushed weight all across the world. So again, there was no need to ask what was a man like him doing in a party like this.

"Can you buy my drink?" he asked, flashing a sexy smile.

"You don't need me to buy you a drink." I flirted back.

"Nah, I don't," he chuckled. "Let me buy you a drink when you're done with that."

"Sure." I smiled bashfully. This man was too damn fine and the scent of his cologne had me woozy. "I'll come find you when I'm ready for that drink."

"Ima hold you to that." Again, he smiled. I quickly walked away because I needed to get away from this man. He had me so smitten, I nearly lost focus on my mission. And this was the reason I didn't have a man. I really didn't have time for one nor did I have time to date. In the line of work I was in, there were no distractions and relationships were just that.

Heading back into the open space where everyone was in tune with the party, I stopped the waitress that had walked by.

"Excuse me, can you give this to Mr. Acosta? His wife won't seem to leave his side." I winked at her and she instantly caught on. I handed her the champagne bottle and glass that I had already poured. Thanking her, I walked away and blended into the crowd. From where I stood I had the perfect view of my mark. I watched as the waitress tapped his shoulder. She whispered something to him and he openly took the bottle and glass from the tray. He nodded his head to her and she scurried off into the crowd.

As I sat back watching Acosta, I could feel a pair of eyes watching me. I turned to look in the direction and the sexy gentleman from the bar was watching me. For a brief moment we locked eyes and it felt like no one was in the room but us. Again, he bit into that bottom lip as fire burned in his eyes. I thought of the things

I would do to him and I got lost in a sexual fantasy. I was so consumed with my thoughts I never heard the mere chatter. I focused my attention back on Acosta and just that fast he was laid out on the marble floor. His wife was kneeled down beside him, screaming out in agony, as the fire from the fire pit burned behind them.

When I looked back over to the mysterious guy, his attention was focused on the scene in front of him. It's like he felt me watching him because he looked up and we instantly locked eyes. I smiled one last time because my job here was done. I headed out of the party and handed the valet my ticket. I waited only five mintes before they brought me the car. Climbing in, I reached into my purse and handed the man a tip. I then closed my door and got ready to pull out of the driveway. Before I made it completely out, the same guy had run out of the party in hopes to catch me but it was too late. I peeled out into the streets and blended in with the traffic. I pulled out my phone and sent a text to Frank that the job was done. I laid my head back on the seat and the mysterious guy crossed my mind. Had this been another lifetime, I would have been rolling over in my McLaren sheets making love to him until the sun came up. But this was reality and in my reality, love doesn't exist.

Three

Queen

Two weeks later...

I looked through the scope of my Glock 19 and focused on my target. Slightly closing my eyes, I fell into that dark place that abruptly taunted my heart. I pictured my parents' killers and although I didn't have a face, I made one up in my mind.

Pop! Pop! Pop! Pop! Pop! Pop! Pop! Pop! Pop! Pop! Pop! Pop!
Pop! Pop! Pop! Pop! Pop! Pop! Pop! Pop! Pop! Pop! Pop!
Pop! Pop! Pop! Pop! Pop! Pop! Pop! Pop! Pop!

I pulled the trigger until all 33 bullets from my factory magazine were gone. Peering up at my target, I slightly smirked because I had two headshots and all the rest were upper torso. I pulled off my face goggles, and the sound of someone clamping pulled my attention. Quickly pulling my 380 glock from my waist, I turned around only to be met with Franko.

"Whoa, whoa, Queen, it's me."

"Franko." I let out a sigh, clutching my chest. He pulled out a cigarette and put flame to it before speaking. "You'll kill a motherfucker before the blink of an eye. I taught you well my child," he said and stepped over to me. We both looked over the rubber made statue and examined each bullet hole.

"What brings you by?" I asked as I began to reload my gun.

"Have something important to talk to you about."

"I'm listening," I spoke as I put the last bullet into my magazine.

"I have a hit. It's not like just any hit. This one is very personal," he spoke, taking a pull from his cigarette.

"So what's so special about this one that you had to show up here?"

"Well, my child, this man is treacherous. Hood nigga, moves with caution, and always ten steps ahead. He doesn't trust anyone, however, he is a ladies' man. And oh does the ladies love him." Again, he took a hit from his cigarette, dropped it and used his Ashley Stenson loafers to put it out. "This one's gonna take some time. Another hit from the mayor. We have a couple months to get it done."

"Why so long?"

"You have to get close to him. Build his trust." Frank looked at me, trying hard to read me.

"Why can't I just knock him off like I do everyone else?"

"It's not that easy, Queen. God damn it, don't be such a bull." The wrinkles in his forehead formed. I was as *Treacherous* as they come and right now Franko was insulting my character.

Pop! Pop! Pop! Pop! Pop!

With my gun smoking in my hand, I turned to look back at Franko. He wore a galvanized look. His eyes were trained on the statue that I had only fired five bullets into. Two eye shots, one chest shot, one bullet to the middle of the head and one to the dick that I had done purposely.

"Trust me, he ain't fucking with me." I smirked with confidence. I had this shit in a bag and if Franko didn't know by now he would never know. Just two weeks ago I killed one of the most powerful men that plenty of men gunned for but couldn't get close enough to kill. However, one pill and a glass of champagne was all it took. So again, I had this shit in a bag.

***

As I watched John's home, I looked down at my watch. It was nearly 11pm and right on cue his wife was exiting the home. I watched as she climbed into her car and it disappeared into the night. Biting into my bottom lip, I peered up to the window of John's bedroom. The flicker from the television was evident he was in his room. I strutted across the street unable to contain myself. I needed my fix and I needed it now. With each step I took, the sound of my Marc Jacob heels clicked along the pavement. When I made it to the side of his home, I used the branch that hung from the tree and flipped myself onto the wooden log that was nailed into his home. I then gripped the electricity wiring tightly and used it to pull myself up to the second level. This was how I always entered.

"Baby girl," he called out to me. This was the pet name he gave me because he didn't know my name.

"I've missed you too," I spoke seductively and climbed through. Without wasting time, I unraveled my long trench coat and let it fall to the ground. That same fire that was always in his eyes nearly set my body into flames. I lifted my dress and exposed my naked body. John loved when I wore no panties. "Come here, sexy." I motioned with my finger seductively. He slid his body down to the edge of the bed as he watched me. I climbed on top of him and without much force I entered him inside of me. See, John was about an average size seven. Because I rarely had sex I had to make it work, which is why I was always the aggressor. Now don't get me wrong, I was sexually attracted to him and not to mention he was undeniably gorgeous, however, this was sex and sex only.

"Can you at least...?"

"Shhhh." I used my hand to cover his mouth. I continued to ride him like a kentucky derby. His mouth fell into an O and his eyes began to roll to the back of his head. I stayed in this same position and rode him for nearly thirty minutes before he finally reached his peak. I could feel his semen oozing out of him as he began to bite into my shoulder. With him still inside of me, I kissed him nice, long and passionately. I stood to my feet and pulled down my dress, leaving him breathing hard.

"Baby girl," he spoke in between breaths. With one leg out of the window, I turned to face him. "When will I see you again?" he asked with sorrow etched on his face.

"Soon," I replied attentively and then turned to look away. I scanned the perimeter and made a dash for it; and just like that, I had vanished into the night air.

Four

Queen

Walking into Franko's home, I was greeted by his maid who you couldn't tell me he wasn't fucking. She spent too much time in his bedroom when his wife was gone and even lurking around his office like she was cleaning. However, it wasn't my business so I never spoke on it. Therefore, I bypassed her and headed down the long hall and up the spiral staircase that led to his office. When I walked inside, he sat behind his desk and just like always he wore an Italian suit that cost a fortune. Frank was paid. Hell, he paid me well, and of course, he got his cut off top. One would think he was part of a drug cartel but no, Franko was a part of a hitman ring. He trained and groomed some of the most treacherous hitmen but I was reigned queen of the throne because of my skills.

Franko swore he taught me everything I knew but that was fiction. I'd run circles around his chubby frame and make him see six of me before his death. I was dedicated to my craft so I was the reason I had learned everything I know. Now don't get me wrong, he taught me moves that would take a person out with a splinter but I taught myself the most important thing—accuracy. I was always accurate when it came to my kills. That shit took dedication, patience and a steady hand.

"Queen, my love, have a seat," he said just as he hung up his call. He pulled the huge manilla envelope from his desk drawer and began pulling photos of whom I assumed this *big hit* as he referred was on. "This is our man," he slid the pictures across the table. I pulled them into my hand and zoomed in on my next mark. I looked from the photos to Franko astonished. It was the same man that had offered me a drink inside of Acosta's event. Although the man was dressed down in simple sweats and a white tee, I knew that smile from anywhere.

"Queen," he called out to me, bringing me from an adoring daze.

"Oh huh?"

"Did you hear me?"

"Yes. Sincere," I repeated his name.

"This is Sincere. Remember what I said he's a very dangerous man. He runs everything in Manhattan and even in the Bronx. The streets fear him," he spoke settled.

"What's the plan?" I dropped the photos on his desk, still electrified.

"Acosta's funeral. He'll be there." I nodded my head in agreement.

"When is it?"

"Two days. They just released his body." Again, I nodded and he continued to give me the details about Sincere.

"Queen, you have to take this hit slow. Don't rush because we don't wanna alarm him. Take your time, love." He looked at me to make sure I understood. "The job pays a quarter of a million dollars so you can't fuck this up."

"I have it under control." I stood from my seat.

"That's my girl." He smiled and pulled his cigarette from his package.

"Anything else?"

"Be careful," he replied, looking me in the eyes. I gave him one head nod and made my way towards the door. "Queen, be careful." Again, he called out but I continued out the door, bumping right into Nelly.

"Oh, excuse me, Queen."

"It's okay, Nelly." I smiled and headed up the hall. Nelly headed into his office and closed the door behind herself. *Some maid,* I thought as I let myself out the door. Again, it wasn't my business but Lord if Jizzle got wind she was gonna kill them both. Jizzle was no joke. She was actually a retired hitman which is how they had met. I guess the saying is true, you lose them how you get him. Because Jizzle started off as a side chick and moved up to become the first lady. Before her, there was Natalie, his ex-wife who ended up dead mysteriously. I don't know why but I had a feeling Jizzle's name was written across it. But once again, it wasn't my business.

"Ashes to ashes, dust to dust; in sure and certain hope of the Resurrection to eternal life, through our Lord Jesus Christ."

As the pastor recited the bible scripture the sound of Acosta's wifes weeps filled the air. She wiped her tears with a cloth as everyone stood around consoling her. The pastor then released twenty two doves into the sky that began to circle around us then suddenly flew away. As the family dropped their roses on the casket I fell into a tainting daze. This was the same cemetery my parents were buried and I hadn't visited in nearly a year. A lone tear slid down my face as that day played vividly through my mind.

"So we meet again." I paused because the voice was too familiar. Slowly turning around, I came face to face with Sincere. Just like at the party he wore a ravishing suit and his hair was freshly twisted. This time he had it hanging loosely all over his head. Wiping the tear from my eye, I smiled warmly, making him smile along.

"It's aight, ma." He reached out to grab my chin.

"It's so sad," I lied, trying my best to sound convincing.

"Yeah, shit cold." He looked off just as the truck lifted Acostas casket into the ground.

"Well, it's nice seeing you again. I have to go."

"Nah, you ain't getting away from me again." He pulled me by the arm and stopped me in my tracks.

"What you mean?" I blushed slyly.

"I mean, I can't let you get away again, ma. You gotta let me take you out or something."

"Uhhh, I don't know about that. My life is complicating right now." I sighed, playing it off.

"Not as complicated as it was for me to approach you. Shit, I was nervous as hell, girl." He flashed those pearly white teeth.

"Okay, I'll give you my number. I'm not sure about when I'll be able to go out but at least we can get to know each other. Just be patient, okay?"

"Ima tell you now, I don't have patience. Anything I want, I get, and trust me, Ima have yo sexy ass," he spoke cockily—so sure of himself. *And there goes my panties.*

"What's your name, ma?"

"Well, it ain't, ma." I smirked, making him laugh. "Queen." I extended my hand. To my surprise, he took it into his and kissed it. Right then, the sound of his phone rang. He motioned for me to give him one minute and that was perfect because I had to recollect myself.

Shortly after, Sincere walked back over to me tucking his phone into his top pocket. I could tell the call had to be urgent because he moved eagerly.

"I gotta run, shorty, but hit me aight?" I nodded my head yes and again he rubbed my chin. "You be easy, Queen." He flashed that smile before heading over to a Lamborghini Centenario. I watched as the car pulled away before I decided to head out. The moment I hopped into my car, my phone rang. Knowing it was Franko, I let it go to voicemail. I needed to gather myself before speaking to him. Letting out a sigh, I knew this mission was gonna be hard. However, this is what I signed up for so work had to be done.

Five

Sincere

"You thought you were gone, get away with this shit! Huhhh, bitch ass nigga!"

"Sin, stop pleeeease. You're gonna kill him!"

"Watch out, Keyshia."

"No please. I'll pay you back for him. Please, I'll give you everything I have." Hearing Keyshia say those words stopped me in my tracks. I turned to look at her as I huffed and puffed.

"You got 60 bands to give me?" I fumed. Her eyes bucked but she didn't say a word.

"Exactly." I turned back to this nigga Cordell. "Nigga, on my wife, you got three days to run me my bread."

He looked at me with his mouth and nose leaking. I looked down at my brand new Margiela's and noticed a speck of blood. I wanted so badly to turn around and bash his head in again. He was lucky all these witnesses were out here or he would have been dead. My trigga finger was itching right now but I couldn't take the chance. Therefore, I headed to my whip and pulled off before I changed my mind. I was furious. One thing I didn't play about was my wife or my money. Shit, other than my mother, those were the only two things I loved in this world.

I didn't have kids because Helen couldn't reproduce. She had a disease called preeclampsia that affected her ability to birth a child. She had been pregnant twice and each time, had a sudden increase in blood pressure so after the 20th week of pregnancy, the baby always passed. She always said she was okay but I knew that was a lie because of the way she always looked at women with their children. Even her best friend Freya's daughter who was four, stayed at our crib more than her own home. Little girl loved the fuck out of me too. I couldn't front, a nigga wanted kids so I often told Helen we could adopt. She always declined and hit me with "I don't want kids." And again, I knew that was a lie.

Stepping into my crib, I called out for my wife until I realized she was out shopping with Freya. As I crossed the threshold to my bedroom, I stopped to take in the picture of Helen that had been hand painted by an artist named Michelle Morgan. The painting looked like a spit image of my wife even down to the one dimple on her left cheek. Everytime I looked at the picture, it would bring me a sense of peace. And this was why I loved my wife to death. A nigga was insidious in these grimy streets so after a long day I'd come home and she would put my mind at ease.

Heading into my room, I was actually happy she wasn't here. I needed to rid my bloody shirt and change out these bloody shoes. Anytime she saw blood she would began to worry and a nigga didn't need that; especially after the day I just had. This nigga Cordell was one of my workers that I trusted with my bread. He was the only nigga in Harlem that held the biggest sack. Now I don't wanna get to jumping to conclusions on why my money was gone because I'm not one to throw a jacket on niggas or listen to rumors. However, one of my other workers Santo had mentioned him moving funny. Santo swore the nigga was on dope but again I wasn't one to put a jacket on nobody. His business was his business and after he gave me my bread then his spot was being handed over.

Stepping into the shower, I let the steaming hot water run down me. Letting out a sigh, I spun around so the water could hit my back. Suddenly little mama crossed my mind. *Queen.* I thought, imagining her sexy ass smile. Never in my entire four years of marriage have I stepped out on my wife. Everywhere I went bitches threw themselves at me but I never did it. Not only because of Helen's feelings but I didn't trust these hoes. However, it was something 'bout this Queen chick I found intriguing. She was the sly type and just the look in her eyes told me she had a whole ass story behind her. I didn't have any intentions of fucking shorty but I found it odd how we kept bumping heads. It's like the shit was a sign and with the type of instinct I possessed, I wasn't gonna just ignore it.

"Oh, niggas taking showers by they self?" Helen's silhouette stood behind the glass door. This was something we always said anytime one of us hopped into the shower without each other. I slid the glass back and my eyes darted over to my bloody shirt. *Damn.* Helen looked in the direction and stepped closer to examine it. She picked it up and then looked at me with that same worried look she always gave me.

"What's this?"

"Man, I'm here, right?" I really didn't wanna be bothered with this.

"By the grace of God. Sincere, you ain't gone learn until something in them streets happened to yo black ass."

"And you ain't gone learn to stop jinxing a nigga!" I shot. I hated when she did that shit. I been in the game since my freshman year of high school and I made it this far. She slammed the shirt into the ground and stormed out the restroom. *She got me fucked up.* I hopped out and left the shower running.

"Man, you gone fix that attitude, ma. You know what the fuck I do for a living so you know I got shit to handle in these streets. You see all them fucking bags." I pointed to the many bags that aligned the floor. There were two Gucci bags, a Saks bag and a whole bunch of other shit I know cost a grip. "You wanna continue to live like this then let me live yo. A muthafucka stole 60 bands from me so I had to handle my fucking business!" She looked up at me with that puppy dog ass look she always gave me but nah not today. "Don't give me that fucking look because the shit ain't gone work."

"You got workers to handle that type of shit for you. I just don't want nothing to happen to you."

"I understand that but I gotta handle shit myself. That's why this nigga was comfortable with doing the shit because he expected me to let my workers deal with it. This was a nigga I trusted and been trusting so guess what? Them *let my workers deal with it* days are over. You think my reputation in these streets came from letting my workers deal with shit?"

"Baby, I know. And that's the thing, you have a rep out there. Muthafuckas know you not to be played with so you don't have to prove nothing to nobody. If something happens to you, Sincere, I'll have nothing. You're all I got!" She burst out into tears. Now see this was the shit I hated. Helen hated my lifestyle but what she failed to realize is, I would go against God to make it back home to her. I made sure to move cautiously in these streets rather the streets fear me or not.

"Man, stop crying and shit, ma, I'm straight. Trust me." I demanded she look at me. We made eye contact and her face softened. "Trust me," I added and she nodded her head. I kissed her on the lips and headed back into the restroom to finish my shower. This girl had a nigga worked up really over nothing. Cordell wasn't a threat to me and that nigga just like anybody else knew my get down. And since he wanted to test me, I was gonna show him that he forgot who I the fuck I was. Helen had to deal with it.

Stepping out of the shower, I dried off and wrapped a towel around my waist. I stepped into my bedroom reluctantly and Helen was still sitting in the same spot. That disappointed look she wore before I left was now replaced with lust. Her eyes roamed over the budge in my towel and then up to my chest. I knew exactly what she was thinking.

"You want some of this dick, yo ass gotta stop trippin'." I let my towel fall to the ground. She eyed my dick like it was the last piece of meat on earth. I leaned up against the wall because if she wanted it, she had to come get this muthafucka.

Helen strolled over to me, dropped to her knees and grabbed my dick. She began licking the tip of it and then moved down the shaft. "Suck that muthafucka," I told her, tired of all the licking.

She looked up at me seductively and then took my entire dick into her mouth. She never took her eyes off me and she began bobbing her head, creating her own rhythm. I bit into my bottom lip because already she had my toes throwing up gang signs. I laid my head back on the wall and grabbed her head. She loved when I did this. I began moving in and out her mouth like I was fucking her pussy and she began gagging. One would think with her gagging she'd beg for me to stop, but nah, she liked that shit. So giving her what she wanted, I pounded in and out her mouth, trying hard to catch my nut. Just the thought of her swallowing it made my dick grow bigger and began pulsating.

She began moving her head side to side like she was gargling my dick and this shit drove a nigga wild. My whole dick was down her throat and trust me I ain't have a little dick. A nigga was blessed in that department, just like Helen was blessed with sucking dick. Never in my life had a bitch been able to make me nut in only ten minutes but Helen. She made her jaws do some shit I called a vacuum and this helped her suck every drop of nut out of me.

"Fuuuuuuck!" a nigga yelled out not being able to help it. By the time she was done, my legs felt like Jell-O. I was still laid against the wall, trying to catch my breath. When I looked down, Helen had a wide grin like she just won an award for the best head ever. I shook my head and helped her stand to her feet. However, she had me all the way fucked up.

"Bend that ass over," I told her and smacked her on the ass. I was about to beat the lining out her pussy and make her submit. With the head she had given me, I felt like I was on the losing end and I couldn't go out like that.

Six

Queen

Tired of Franko calling, I finally decided to pick up the phone and call Sincere. I dialed his number and my stomach began to do somersaults as my heart pounded in my chest. After four rings I went to hang up and damn I heard his masculine voice say, "Hello?"

"Um...can I speak to Sincere?"

"Girl, this ain't no damn house phone and we ain't in junior high," he laughed, making me giggle along.

"My bad." I continued to laugh.

"What's up with you, baby girl? I thought you forgot about me."

"I didn't think you were worried about me calling."

"Hell yeah, shit, I thought I was gone have to come and find you."

"I'm here now." I smiled delightfully.

"Is that right?" I pictured him, nodding his head with that sexy ass smirk. "What you doing right now? You got time to talk?"

"Ummm, just laying here right now. Sure."

"What you got on right now?"

"Boy." I laughed out, making him laugh again.

"Nah, I'm just fucking with you. But real shit, though, what's up with you? I wanna take you out get to know you over a nice candlelight or something."

"Is that right? It sounds good but I'll have to think about it."

"Word, you gon' play me to the left like that," he chuckled.

"Not like that, I just be busy. Not only that it's just been a minute since I've dated."

"And that's the problem, I wanna pull you out that shell. It's a whole ass world out here for us to fuck up, ma. Don't waste your life laying there."

"Okay. How about Saturday?"

"Any day is fine with me. I'll put everything to the side for you."

"Is that right?" I blushed.

"Hell yeah. You got that, baby girl."

"Ima hold you to it."

"Do that. But look, though, I gotta roll out. Ima hit you later on, if that's cool with you."

"Yeah, it's fine."

"Aight, you be sweet."

"I'll try."

"Yeah, okay," he challenged, followed by a light chuckle. The phone went silent but he hadn't disconnected. After a couple seconds, I decided to hang up. I laid my head back on my head board and fell into a slight daze. This mission on Sincere would be harder than I thought. Franko said we had a few months but I wanted to get it over with as soon as possible because I didn't wanna slip up and really start liking him. He seemed like a cool guy, which was puzzling as to why the mayor wanted him dead. But y'all know my motto *ain't my business*.

Date night...

It was the night of my date with Sincere and I was a nervous wreck. After just slicing a man's throat for 30 grand, I was now in a damn pair of heels like I was sinless. Sincere text the address to the restaurant near Rikers Island called Piccola. I guess he was serious about a candlelight dinner because this was a fancy establishment suitable for a date. He said that he would be there by eight sharp and this was perfect because it gave me enough time to calm my damn nerves. I headed into my kitchen and reached under my cabinet for a bottle of Johnnie Walker Scotch. I pulled a shot glass from my cabinet and poured me two shots throwing them back to back. I looked down at my watch and when I noticed it was 7:20, those damn butterflies came back. I quickly took another shot and waited for the liquor to take effect; meanwhile I headed into my room to grab my belongings and then headed for my car.

Pulling up to the restaurant, I noticed a sleek black McLaren 720S, and I knew it couldn't have belonged to anyone but Sincere. Pulling behind him, I killed my engine and climbed out to head inside. When I walked into the establishment, it was pretty busy but it had a romantic feel. The soft music played from the live piano and the dim lights gave it an alluring vibe.

"Yes, ma'am, are you looking for someone?" the hostess addressed me.

"Yes, I'm looking for a Sincere." I began to fidget because I didn't know his last name.

"Yes, Mr. Ingram is right this way." She smiled and guided me to the back. "And stop fidgeting, you look beautiful," she whispered before we reached Sincere's table.

"Thank you." I smiled as she pulled my chair out for me to sit. The smell of his cologne lingered in the air but I was scared to look in his direction.

"Look at me," he demanded. I looked at him nervously and let out a breath that I had been holding so I could get a grip on myself. "Why are you so damn shy around me?" he asked, looking me in the eyes.

"I'm not shy." I dropped my head because his eyes were too damn demanding.

"Queen, look at me, ma. I'm not gon' say it again."

Again, I looked at him but I didn't say a word. Instead I tried to match his look in hopes I'd intimidate him as much as he intimidated me.

"Would you like something to drink?" A waitress walked over just in time.

"Let me get a bottle of Chateau Cheval, and can you bring some Calamari and Prawn cocktails."

"Yes, sir, coming right up." She scurried away to put in Sincere's order.

"Are you always so demanding, Sincere?" I asked, trying hard to break the ice.

"It's the only way I could be. The world is mine, ma," he spoke so cocky that my love box thumped so loud I prayed he didn't hear it.

"What sign are you?" I smiled, assuming he had to be a Leo.

"I'm a Leo, and you?"

"I'm a Libra." I tried hard not to laugh. This was something I always did since young. Even when I went on hits I'd always ask Franko to find out their sign. He always told me I was foolish but to me I was ten steps ahead. I used this to know my victim's weaknesses, strengths and who I was dealing with. Like now, I knew that Leo men were very arrogant with big hearts. A Leo's heart was so big that you would look past all their flaws.

"So you got a birthday coming up?"

"Yep." I half smiled, thinking about my birthday. I haven't celebrated a birthday in years. Most of the time I was so consumed in my work I forgot it was even my big day.

"So can I get first dibs on taking you out?" he asked, bringing me from my thoughts.

"I don't know about that. It's a month away and after this date you might dump me." I smirked.

"Or you might dump me." We joined each other for a laugh. "Nah, but real shit, I wanna get to know you. What type of shit you like to do? Favorite movie, favorite place in the world, shit like that."

"I don't have a problem with that. But let me start by asking you some questions." He nodded his head for me to ask along. I had so many questions, however, I didn't wanna come off as nosey." Just as he was gonna answer, the waitress walked over with the wine and appetizers. She sat everything down on the table and Sincere looked up at her.

"I don't want this wine. Please bring me another one that's not open," he told her seriously. She looked at him as if she didn't understand. He said it again but the second time with much more force. Just hearing him say this made me begin to fidget in my seat. *He's always ten steps ahead*, I thought of Franko's words and I saw what he meant.

"Okay, I'll be right back," she spoke nervously but Sincere was unmoved. He thanked her and actually smiled. I let out a soft sigh because Sincere just made my job harder than it already was.

Seven

Sincere

"Don't look like that, baby girl. I don't mean to seem offensive, I just don't trust shit. I didn't ask her to open my shit she could have just brought it to me."

"Yeah, I feel you, no one can be trusted these days."

"You're right about that." I pulled a shrimp from the glass jar and took a bite. I know Queen thought I was bugging out but shit I didn't even trust the cocktail sauce. "So what was yo questions?" I asked, picking up where we left off.

"Huh? Oh my bad. Umm...I just wanted to know about your background. Like are you in a relationship, kids, things like that."

"No relationship and no kids," I lied. I wanted so badly to tell her about Helen but I didn't wanna run her off. She looked like the type of chick that didn't fuck with married men but eventually I'd tell her.

"What's your favorite movie?"

"Harlem Nights. Yours?"

"Dirty Dancing."

"Patrick Swayze." I smiled, thinking 'bout the movie. I watched that shit with my moms when I was younger. I could vividly hear my moms saying how sexy the white guy was. "What about you? I ain't gone be having no niggas gunning for me and shit, right?" I smirked, awaiting her answer.

"No, no, men."

"I find that hard to believe as sexy as you are." She instantly began blushing with her shy ass. Shit was kind of cute.

"Thank you."

"So what is it you do for a living?"

"I'm a...ummm real estate agent."

"That's what's up, maybe you can hook me up with a crib."

"You got that." She smiled and grabbed a shrimp from the glass. We continued our questions and the more we talked, the more I found her intriguing. Her conversation was so bomb that we lost track of time. It was Saturday night and because I came and went as I pleased I didn't have anywhere to rush off too. Queen was a breath of fresh air for a nigga so spending an entire night with her was fondly.

I flagged the waitress down and gave her the money for the food. Shortly after she came back with the to-go bag from Queen. After eating the shrimp and calamari, she barely touched her food so we bagged it up. We both stood to our feet and I made eye contact with the detail that was seated off to the side, blending in with the patrons. Queen looked around and then back to me and slightly shook her head. Sooner or later she would understand who I was and the way I moved.

Heading out of the restaurant, Queen latched onto my arm unexpectedly. I could tell she was a little buzzed from the wine and it was a good thing because she had finally loosened up. When we stepped out into the air, it was breezy but calm. I turned to look at her hoping she'd stay out for a while and a nigga got lost in her beauty for a slight mintue. The wind blew through her so she tucked a loose strand behind her ear and then looked around nervously.

"You turning it in?" I asked her, hoping she'd say no.

"Yeah, I have to get up early."

"On a Sunday?"

"Yes, I have to um...wash and clean up. You know, get things together for Monday. Sundays are pretty much a chill day for me but I have to prepare for the week."

"Yeah, I understand. I normally stay in and watch football. It's the only day out of the week I really can relax."

"Well, I had a nice time." She faintly smiled. I pulled her chin into my hand and lightly rubbed it. I felt like I was in high school and this was my first date ever. I wanted so badly to kiss her but I didn't wanna seem thirsty. We watched each other for a slight moment but neither one of us said a word.

"I...I..I'll see you, I'll see you tomorrow," she fumbled over her words. However, I didn't break our eye contact.

"Do I make you nervous, Queen?" I asked her on a more serious note. She didn't answer but her eyes spoke volumes. "Keep shit real." I looked at her and paused. "You should be. I'm a dangerous guy with a monster of a dick." I stepped up closer to her. Again, I grabbed her chin to make sure she didn't look away. "You should be nervous because when I get a hold of you, Ima have you going in circles. And I always get what I want." I don't know if I was tripping, but when she closed her eyes, a soft moan escaped her lips. And with that, I turned to head for my whip, leaving her relishing in the moment.

Watching her from my whip, baby girl looked like she was floating on cloud fifty. The way she looked at me alone, I could tell she wanted a nigga. Something in the pit of my stomach told me I'd be craving this chick effortlessly. However, I prayed she could keep a secret because this shit couldn't get back to my wife. This was one of the reasons I didn't fuck around. Daily women through pussy my way but I knew how women got down. They waited to make a fool out of your wife, but I wasn't gonna give them the satisfaction.

I looked through the rearview and caught the last glimpse of Queen. She was still sitting there like she was trying to decide what to do. I don't know why but a slight jealousy came over me, wondering if she was gonna run to the next nigga. I mean, I asked him she had a dude and she swore she didn't. Even if she had male friends she could keep it buck with me and I'd still fuck with her. Not liking what this chick was doing to me, I pulled off and headed home to my wife. The entire time she invaded my thoughts. I wanted to know more about her and even get next to her. But for now I was gonna play shit cool. I was gonna show her that I could be patient although I felt like we were both grown and we should just do us.

When I pulled up to my crib I headed inside and straight for the shower. Once I was done, I went into my office so I could handle some work and check on my bread. Because I didn't have a legit business I never understood why I had a damn office, but for the first time it came in handy. I didn't want to face Helen. Or at least not yet. A nigga was still caught up over my date with Queen, I needed a moment to myself.

I laid my head back on my office chair and the vision of Queen in that dress made my dick rise.

We were in my bedroom with candles lit and some of that girly shit playing in the background. I walked up on her and wasted no time removing her dress. It fell to the ground causing me to stop and lust over her curves. When she looked up at me, her eyes pleaded for me to continue; so I did just that. I began tracing kisses on her neck and down to her breast. She took my dick into her hand and began stroking it nice and slow. My dick grew to its biggest and I could feel the pulse thumping in the palm of her hands.

"Fuck me," she spoke above a whisper and right when I laid her on the bed...

"Honey, come to bed," the sound of Helen's voice brought me from my daze. I opened my eyes as I cursed myself for not locking the door. She had just fucked up a perfectly good fantasy. Shit, I was trying to see if I could fuck shorty.

"I'll be down in a minute."

When she walked out, I waited for a brief moment and then picked up my phone. I went to Queen's number and placed the call. I was really iffy about Facetime calls but I needed to see her.

Moments later, surprisingly, she answered the phone. Without saying a word, I looked at her background and I could tell she was home. My eyes fell down to the cream silk gown she wore that exposed her hard nipples.

"I was just making sure you took yo ass home."

"Oh my God. Why wouldn't I?" she chuckled.

"Shit, maybe yo little boo or something."

"Aww, let me find out you jealous." She smirked, making me laugh.

"Nah, ma, I ain't sweating it because when I make you mines you ain't gone want them other niggas."

"You really so sure of yourself, huh?"

"Confidence, baby." Again, I made her laugh. To my surprise we continued to talk. We actually stayed on the phone for an hour after. By the time I headed downstairs to Helen she was sound asleep, which was good because I wanted to replay the conversation I had with Queen in my mind. *This was gonna be a long night.* I let out a sigh and climbed into the bed. I turned to my side so my back would be to Helen. A nigga was so guilty I couldn't face her.

Eight

Queen

After my date with Sincere, I headed home feeling elatedly. A part of me wanted to stay and hang out with him but I was too damn scared. Our date was so refreshing that I found myself blissfully intrigued with him. I hated that I would have to kill him because he was really a nice guy. Although he was very vulgar and intimidating, he meant well by it. Sincere was the type of man to get what he wanted and he didn't bite his tongue about it either. Last night we talked on Facetime for over an hour and I actually enjoyed his conversation. We talked about all types of things, even the things I found myself researching that were weird, like aliens for instant. I had an infatuation with outer space and life beyond humans. Imagine my surprise when he mentioned The Fourth Kind.

Not only that but he talked dirty to me, making me nearly soak my bed. And thanks to him, I was now sitting in front of John's home, waiting for his wife to leave. It was Sunday morning, which meant she worked part time for four hours. Her normal shift was graveyard but on Sundays she worked the day. Sitting in one spot for sometime she had finally emerged from the home and climbed into her car. I watched as the car drove down the street before I stepped out of my car and slightly jogged up the street.

"Hello, sexy," I cooed as I entered John's bedroom window. He quickly turned to me and his eyes pleaded he missed me. He stood from the chair already knowing what I had come for. He eyed the long trench coat that I wore and he knew I wasn't wearing any panties. As he bit into his bottom lip, I untied the jacket seductively and let it fall to the floor. I then walked over to his bed and bent over so we don't waste any more time. I needed to feel him now. Because he was already shirtless, he removed his pants and then followed by his briefs. He joined me on the bed, dick already reaching its highest hard. Latching onto his arm around my waist, he pulled me into him. In one swift move, he entered me and then collapsed on my back.

"Oooh, I love you," he spoke into my ear. I closed my eyes and pictured it was Sincere who had spoken those words. As John began to stroke me, the sound of a woman's voice could be heard through the home. Because the sound was so close it was evident that his wife had already climbed the stairs.

"Shit!" He jumped up and slid into his pants. I quickly threw on my jacket but I didn't have time to make it out of the window. I quickly jumped into his closet, and found myself bunched up with plenty male suits. I closed my eyes in hopes she didn't discover me hiding. I knew it was possible the smell of sex that lingered in the air but John would have to explain that.

"I decided to just take off today. I was gonna just go get my hair done but I forgot your credit cards." I listened to her speak as she moved around the room. I never heard John's voice but I did hear movement as if she had walked out of the door. Shortly after, the closet door opened and when John's face appeared, I let out a deep sigh.

"That was close," I told him and headed for the window. As badly as I wanted to let off a few nuts, I decided to leave because that was too risky. As I put one leg out the window, the sound of John's voice roaring stopped me in my tracks.

"Wait a minute, dammit!"

I turned around and the veins in his neck were popping out.

"I'm getting really tired of this. You come, you fuck me and leave. I'm falling in love with you and I don't even know your damn name!" He held onto his blonde strands of hair as if he was gonna snatch them out. The room fell silent as I watched the pain in his eyes. *He fell in love,* I thought, watching this poor man's despairing facial expression. We continued to lock eyes and for the first time I was left speechless. Although our attraction for one another was rapturous, it was only sex and nothing much more.

"Queen," I finally spoke, filling the silence and there was nothing else to say.

"Queen," he mumbled my name. Again, we held each other's gaze and then I made a dash for it. I leapt from the second story landing on my feet. I headed up the street and with every step I felt someone watching me. I turned around and John stood in his window with his eyes trained on me. I quickly ducked off into someone's yard and hit a few fences to get to my car. When I reached it, I climbed in and sat there for a split moment. I took in what had just happened and I was grateful we didn't get caught. I couldn't be the cause of John losing his family because I couldn't fill that void. I wasn't the woman for him because we lived in two totally different worlds, so after today, I was gonna take more precautions.

"So where are we going?"

"It's a surprise." Sincere looked over from his seat and smirked.

It's been four days since our first date and Franko insisted I go out with him again. He said that I had to get close to Sincere and being distant wasn't gonna help the hit. What he didn't know was, I was distant for a reason. I was beginning to like this man and every day that went by it began to get harder. We talked everyday, even three, maybe four times a day. He would always send me a cute little text that had become a part of our daily routine. Not only was he so damn handsome, he had great conversation, and his cocky persona drove me crazy.

As we pulled into Central Park, I noticed all the cars and people that flooded the parking lot. Sincere swooped his car into the empty stall and eagerly climbed out. He wore this huge goofy grin, looking like an excited child. When I climbed out of the car, Sincere walked over to me and pulled my hand into his. We headed into the park and when he retrieved the tickets from the attendant, I looked at him and smiled. The huge sign read *Shakespeare in the Park* and this took me by surprise.

Anyone on the outside looking in, would think that Sincere was a typical hood nigga. However, he had enough class to hold 32 students. His long locks, jewelry and the white tee that fit him perfectly, gave him that thuggish style but when he opened his mouth, his vocabulary was impeccable. So my point is, it didn't surprise me that he brought me to a Shakespeare play. I smiled delightfully and we entered the park and found our seats. Sincere not once let go of my hand and every now and then he would squeeze it tight.

Twenty minutes into the show and I already had tears in my eyes. I loved Shakespeare and especially Romeo & Juliet. Their play never got old to me, no matter how many times I had seen it. Every now and then Sincere looked over at me laughing and he really fell out when I mentioned I had bad allergies. By the time the play was done, my emotions were all over the place. I had seen this play with Cellus years ago so my thoughts were trained on that day.

"Thank you." I smiled, trying hard to gather my thoughts.

"You enjoyed yourself?" he asked and pulled me into his embrace. He buried his head into the nape of my neck, causing me to giggle.

"Yes I did. I love Shakespeare."

"Yeah, I could tell wit' yo cry baby ass," he laughed just as his phone began to ring. He let one arm fall from around my neck and he answered.

"Yo?" he spoke into the phone but he never took his arm from around me. "Aight, I'm on my way," he replied to the caller. The tightness in his jaw told me it was serious but he didn't say a word.

"I'd hate to cut our date short but some shit came up I need to handle," he finally spoke.

"I can go with you if you don't mind." I didn't want our date to be cut short either. Not to mention, I needed to get as close to him as possible so I could complete my mission.

"Like I've told you before, Queen, I'm a very powerful man. My life is very complex and shit might get ugly. I may have to knock a nigga head back." He looked at me to wait for my reaction.

"And what does that have to do with me rolling with you?" *Nigga, I kill for a living.* He looked at me and began contemplating but he didn't say a word.

As we drove through the roughest part of NY, I sat in the passenger seat fumbling with my phone. From time to time I could feel Sincere's eyes glance over at me. He now had his pistol sitting on his lap but again he held my hand into his. I could tell he looked for someone because he turned down several streets and when he didn't see them, he would pull off and head for another location.

His phone constantly rang but he never bothered to answer. That was another way I knew that whatever it was was serious. He always answered his phone except for when his little boo called. I wasn't no dummy, I knew when a woman called because he would look at it then his whole demeanor would slightly change. I never bothered calling him out on it because of course this fine ass man had women. I was sure they flocked to him because he was too damn hard to resist. Hell, he had me checking for his ass when I was supposed to be doing a job.

Nine

Sincere

Looking over at Queen I couldn't do shit but shake my head. That innocent, boujie girl shit went straight out the window when she asked if she could ride. Although she was trying to play tough, I hoped like hell I didn't run her off with the type of shit I was involved in like now. I had received a call from Butch telling me Cordell hadn't gave him the bread. Oh, and let me not forget the nigga Cordell's people looking for me and supposed to have a price on my head. I was sure it was his people from Pennsylvania because them niggas had a name. I ain't give a fuck about all that because no nigga pumped fear in my heart, which is why I was on the way.

Another thing I was certain of, was these niggas didn't do their homework on me because I was the most feared nigga in my city. Since the age of 16, I been laying niggas down. Before the age of 18, I had made a name for myself. I could have chosen money over killings but having money wasn't shit if you didn't have respect. I knew plenty niggas from my hood that had bread and got bitch rolled everyday. That would never be a nigga like me.

As Queen and I pulled up to Glen Lane, I scanned the crowd of niggas in search for Cordell. When I didn't see him amongst the crowd, I turned another few blocks, hoping I'd see him. The nigga was nowhere in sight but my nigga Butch flagged me down so I pulled alongside the curb. When I hopped out, Queen also hopped out, making me look over at her like she was crazy.

"Queen, get back into the car, ma." I turned back to holla at Butch.

"Man, that nigga's people been riding through looking for you. Them niggas know damn well you don't hang out so I guess they were trying to send a message."

"I ain't worried. I hope them niggas slide through now." I glanced over my shoulder and shook my head. Queen's hard-headed ass was still outside the whip so as me and Butch continued our conversation I kept a close eye on her.

"So have you seen the nigga at all?"

"Nah, I ain't seen that nigga since the day you whooped his ass."

"Aight." I nodded. Cordell was the type of nigga you had to watch because he for sure would bust a gun. He wasn't no scary nigga, which is why I let him hold the biggest sack out of all my workers. Since the day I met Cordell I had to give it to him because he protected my empire like it was his. He had caught plenty of bodies for me but I was starting to believe he had to be on some power trip shit.

"Man, that nigga might be on that shit. He always looking weird and..." Before he could finish, I turned to check on Queen and I noticed a black Tahoe pull along the side of my whip.

"Watch this car," Butch said just as the passenger window rolled down and a arm reached out.

*Pop! Pop! Pop! Pop! Pop! Pop! Pop! Pop! Pop! Pop! Pop! Pop!
Pop! Pop! Pop! Pop! Pop! Pop! Pop! Pop! Pop! Pop!*

I quickly ducked down behind an old brown Infinity and pulled my strap from my waist line.

*Pow! Pow! Pow! Pow! Pow! Pow! Pow! Pow! Pow!
Pow! Pow! Pow! Pow! Pow! Pow! Pow! Pow!*

I emptied my entire clip off into the Tahoe. To my surprise, they were still shooting, which told me they had come with heavy artillery. *Shit!* I ducked down again and the sound of rapid gunfire could still be heard. Because the shots sounded different, I figured Butch had began opening fire. Suddenly the sound of someone screaming and tires screeching, I knew they had pulled off. I quickly jumped up remembering Queen's dumb ass was out the car. When I looked in her direction, I couldn't believe my fucking eyes. She was holding a gun with ease like she did shooting for a living. She had just let off the last shot towards the fleeing vehicle and it ran into a YMCA building. Astonished, I looked over at Butch and this nigga was hiding behind a car. *Hell nah, can't be.* I thought, knowing damn well it wasn't Queen busting back this entire time.

Astounded, I watched Queen as she tucked her pistol into her back and then looked over in my direction. When she stepped up to me she had a smirk on her face and not one like she had saved me but instead it was more like, *I got them fools*.

"Let's go," she commanded, hearing the sound of sirens approaching.

Snapping out of it, I ran to the whip and we both climbed in. I pulled down the street where the car had been smashed into the building and both niggas were dead. I peered over at Queen and again she hit me with that smirk. I shook my head and then focused my attention on the road. This girl right here, bro, I didn't have no fucking words except I'm in love. The way she handled that gun like it didn't faze her turned me the fuck on. I thought about how Helen tripped off my lifestyle and here it was, a bitch on the same shit I was on. Queen didn't just have a strap; this chick had a strap and knew how to handle that muthafucka. I knew plenty niggas that ain't never shot a gun a day in their life. And trip this, her shit was powerful as fuck. I made a mental note to ask her what type of strap it was and maybe we could do some shit out the ordinary like have a gun conversation. I swear this shit would get my dick harder than it was now.

Pulling into the Ritz Carlton hotel, I looked over to Queen to make sure she didn't object. She looked up from her phone for a split second but said nothing. I wasn't coming here to fuck her or nothing like that, I only came because I had a lot of shit on mind that I couldn't take home. I pulled out my phone and booked the room online. Once I was done, I motioned for her to get out and we headed inside. As we stepped into the hotel the sound of her heels clacking again the towel floor and the way she swayed her hips had a nigga applaud. She held a cold ass game face as if we didn't have a shootout moments prior. We headed to the check in and I handed the receptionist my ID. Moments later, I had the key so we quickly headed up the elevator and to the penthouse suite.

Walking into the room I moved around for a moment then finally got comfortable. I laid on the bed and my eyes instantly darted over to Queen. She still had her shoes on but she joined me on the bed.

"Take yo shoes off, ma. You ain't gotta worry I'm not gone bite yo ass just yet. The way you just bust that strap I gotta take my time with you." I smiled, making her giggle. Man this shit was beyond me. Baby girl was shy as fuck but out here busting guns like she just graduated the National Guard Training Camp.

"Queen, look at me," I demanded because she was into her phone like it was more important.

"I'm sorry." She finally looked up. She dropped her phone into her purse and kicked off her shoes. I looked into her eyes and a nigga got caught up. She had me damn near lost for words and this wasn't me. I was very outspoken and didn't have a shy bone in my body.

"I appreciate what you did but you didn't have to do that."

"You're welcome and yes, I did, Sin." *Damn, she called me Sin.* I smiled to myself because she had used my name on a short term basis. "Look, I know you must think I'm crazy but my life was in danger out there too."

"You're right. I'm just puzzled as to why you carry a gun. You don't seem like the type of chick that needs to walk around with protection."

"I'm not that type of girl; I just have to protect myself." She hit me with a sly grin.

"Man, that shit was sexy as fuck. How you learn to shoot like that?" She began twirling her fingers and looked off into the air.

"A few years back I had a boyfriend that was murdered. He was a good guy, ya know?" She looked me in the eyes to make sure I was paying attention. When I nodded once, she continued, "All we did was step off my front porch on our way to dinner and next thing I know shots rang out. He was killed right before me." Again, she looked off and her face held a sense of dismissal. Whoever this nigga was, it was evident she loved the fuck out of him. "Cellus wasn't street, he didn't owe anybody, he didn't even have enemies. Come to find out, it was an initiation for a gang." She shook her head.

I could tell this was a touchy part of her life but I wanted to know more so I didn't have to paint this picture of her life. I liked Queen. And for some reason, I knew after today I would like her more.

"So is this what taints you?" I asked and she nodded her head yes. "So what's your fears?" Again, she looked away and then looked back at me. I don't know why but this time her eyes were challenging. "Nothing." Her response was calm and steady. "Not even God," she added, blowing me back. Right then, a nigga heart melted. I swear on my unborn seeds, this girl reminded me of a woman version of me. It was actually scary.

"Come here," I told her because there was really nothing left to say. All I wanted to do was wrap my arms around her and hold her close to me. She slid next to me and I took in the scent of her perfume. I had so much shit on my mind but with Queen here she gave me a sense of tranquility. I was gonna paint the city red but right now, I was gonna give her the attention she deserved. However, after tonight, shit was about to get hectic.

Ten

Queen

"**S**hoot him, Queen, you have a clear shot," I coached myself with my hand on the trigger. The pedestrians running, and the cars driving by, everything around me froze. Even with the gunfire that continued to erupt nothing was gonna keep me from killing my target. He was busy shooting at the vehicle that had pulled up and opened fire so he never saw it coming. Just as I was gonna squeeze the trigger, I noticed Sincere had run out of bullets. Knowing I had to save us, I turned my pistol from the clean head shot I had on Sin and began aiming for the truck.

The entire night Sincere slept I was awake lost in my thoughts. Knowing I had a chance to kill him was invading my mind. I feel like I let myself down and I could not care less about what Franko had to say. From time to time I looked over at him and he slept so peacefully. I don't know what was weighing heavy on me more than the fact that I didn't kill him or open up to him about Cellus. When Cellus died, that shit took the little peace of heart I had left. First my parents, then Cellus, it was just too much on my soul. I hated reliving that day so I rarely spoke upon it.

Right now I laid in Sincere's arms and I'd be a damn lie if I said the shit didn't feel good. The entire night he caressed my body but not once did he try and make a move on me. I could tell the shooting from earlier bothered him but he was trying to stay in tune with me. His phone kept ringing nonstop but he looked so peaceful I let him sleep. Just like early this was the perfect chance so I eased my hand to the side of the bed to feel for my gun. When I had the butt gripped firmly I slid it underneath my pillow. Just as I was gonna pull it out Sincere pulled me closer to him and kissed the top of my head. *That was close.*

"Hey, you awake?" I asked to see was he only stirring in his sleep or was he awake.

"Yeah, a nigga can't sleep," he responded when his eyes shot open.

"Your phone has been ringing nonstop."

"It ain't nobody," he replied and wrapped his arms around me tighter. "What time is it?"

"About 3am. Why, do you have somewhere to be?" I asked, fishing for any response of him having someone at home to run too.

"I'm right where I wanna be."

His response took me by surprise. The room fell silent because I didn't know what to say.

"Being with you is like the breath of fresh air I need. From your conversations, the way you look at me and damn the way you shoot a gun, is it safe to say a nigga really feeling you?"

He asked but again I didn't reply. "I don't want you to think I'm moving too fast but I can't help my attraction. Everything about you seems so perfect."

"I'm not perfect, trust me."

"Yeah to you, shit, you everything a man would want and need and that's my opinion." He rolled my body over to make me face him and our lips were inches apart "Like I said, I don't wanna move fast so the ball in your court shorty," his thick full lips spoke, urging me to kiss them. The way he was looking me in the eyes had my panties soaking wet.

I guess Sincere was reading my mind because suddenly he brought his face into mine and kissed my lips softly. He pulled back and looked at me again with those same alluring eyes and then went in to kiss me again. This time he grabbed my head and forced his kiss upon me. His lips were so soft that I got lost in the heat of the moment. I could feel his dick growing and poking me right at my opening. Lord, my tunnel began screaming for him to enter me. Sincere's dick was bigger than John's so I know his love making was superior. When John and I fucked, never did we kiss, so something about right now was much more intense.

"Umm, I think it's time for me to go." I pulled back and wiped my mouth. He hopped up and told me to get myself together to leave. I lifted up off the bed and slid into my shoes. When I grabbed my purse, I stood there nervously. Sincere sat back down and put on his shoes. He then grabbed his phone and began reading his text. I watched him for a slight moment until he looked over at me and then stood to his feet. This man was beyond sexy. It's like he was made perfectly for the face of the earth. I thought about when Franko mentioned him being a ladies' man and I understood why. The way he kissed me and the way his dick felt under his shorts, I wanted to back out of the job. *Damn.*

"Nearly a dozen people have been killed in shootings since Saturday. Behind us is grieving family members who are having a candlelight vigil. We don't know if the killings are gang related at the time but the NYPD is investigating the murders. Amongst the deceased victims, family members have identified 37-year-old Michael Johnson, 24-year-old Allen Walker, and 24-year-old Cordell Phillips. We have no other names at the moment but we'll have more after the investigation."

Ring

The sound of my phone ringing brought me from a daze. I quickly answered and when I heard Franko's voice I knew what the call was about. I continued to peer at the television as Franko began to give me the details of a hit tonight.

"Queen, are you there?"

"Yes, yes."

"Wayne Hung Chu. Tonight."

"Yes, I know, Franko."

"Okay good. How's it going with the other job?"

I let out a slight sigh before answering.

"It's going great, I guess. You were right this man is a hard one."

"I told you so." Franko chuckled. "Just take your time, Queen. And remember don't get too personal. Don't tell him nothing about your life, parents being killed or anything."

"Gotcha," I replied, not understanding why he threw my parents out there but I guess he didn't want me to get that personal.

"Okie dokie."

"Okie dokie." I disconnected the line and fell into another daze. I thought about the news segment and those killings had Sincere's name written all over them. The night we left the hotel had been the last time I saw him. Because he didn't reach out to me, I didn't bother to reach out to him. However, he crossed my mind everyday so today I finally decided to call. I dialed his number and as I waited for him to answer butterflies circulated through my tummy. When his voice came through the phone a lump formed in my throat.

"Sup, sexy?" His voice sounded so damn good.

"Hey," my corny ass replied, making him chuckle. "Ummm...I just wanted to say hey. I haven't heard from you in a few days."

"You miss a nigga?"

"Yes." I didn't hesitate to reply. Although this was a premeditated affair, I actually missed him.

"I miss you too, baby girl. Shit just been hectic around here." He let out a light sigh. Instantly, I knew he was referring to the news.

"Oh okay, well, I didn't wanna to bother you. I just wanted to hear your voice."

"You ain't bothering me, baby. It's a pleasure to talk to you," he replied, making me blush harder. "What's up, ma, can I come scoop you tonight? I need to see you."

"Uh, uh...I have to work," I quickly replied.

"So can I come lay up under you while you work? Come on, Queen, invite a nigga over. You swear you ain't got no nigga so I don't see a problem with me coming."

"Oh my God." I tried laughing so I could quickly think of a reply. "It's not like that. I just have to go to the office and help my boss."

"Yeah, aight, you gone stop playing with me soon," he confidently spoke and we both got silent.

"Hey, can I call you back tomorrow?" I tried to get him off the phone. A bitch was five seconds away from saying "fuck it, pull up."

"Aight, ma, well you have a good night at work."

"Thank you and good night." I pressed end and laid back on my sofa. I wanted so badly to let him know the things I liked about him, like his confidence for one. I also wanted so badly to just say come over and fuck the life out of me. But I couldn't. Granted, this affair was fraudulent, I still wasn't the type of girl to speak my mind. I've been like this since I was a child. I remembered often my mother would always try and come talk to me, I would always keep things bottled up. Growing up, I didn't do the things normal kids did, and that made me grow old so young. My parents were CIA agents so they went out of their way to protect me. I lived in the most fabulous home but I spent all my time locked up in my room. I had a maid, a butler and security that paid me not much attention. By the time I was a teen, I began to crave attention because I wasn't getting it at home, so I started running the gritty streets of New York. Just thinking about my parents made me grab my neck. However, I remembered I didn't have my necklace. I made a mental note to self to search my bedroom because that's the only place it could be.

Sincere: Saturday 3:00 pm sharp

I looked down to my phone and smiled at Sin's message that had randomly come through. Saturday was two days from now, which was perfect. Tonight I had a mission so I could relax tomorrow and prepare. I don't know which one I was more excited about, the hit tonight or my date with Sincere. Either way, they both were a hit that would overload my account.

Eleven

Queen

Two weeks later...

"**S**toooop, Sin." I giggled as Sincere chased me around the hotel room. I jumped onto the bed and grabbed the pillow to defend myself. When he tried to attack me, I began laughing so hard I couldn't even swing. He scooped me into his arms and began tickling me, making me nearly piss my shorts.

"Gimme a kiss and I'll stop."

"Okay, okay." I was still in a fit of laughter. I tried to reach up to kiss him but the way he was holding me he wouldn't let me. I pulled his head down and he instantly began slobbering me down. He then broke our kiss and let me stand to my feet.

Wham!

He smacked me on the ass; he told me to get ready so we can go.

"We just got here." I pouted because we had only been in the room a few hours.

"Come on, sexy, we got shit to do." He smiled at my pouting. I stuck my tongue out and headed for a quick shower.

Over the course of two weeks, Sin and I had been spending nearly every day together. He took me to another play, we had dinner at all the fancy restaurants in the city. Yesterday he surprised me with an AP watch that blew me back. Reluctantly I took the watch because when I said I couldn't accept it he nearly lost it. This morning he picked me up for breakfast so we dined in at *La Shamore* then we came to the hotel to relax. He badgered me about taking him to my home and each time I switched it on him and suggested we go to his house. Each time he got quiet which made me wonder did he in fact have someone.

Another thing I paid attention to was each day we spent together he would always leave. The latest he'd stay out was two maybe three in the morning and this was what men did that had wives. Blowing it off, his personal life was his business because I had a job to do. Each day that went by it became harder for me to kill him, until I would speak to Franko and he would remind me that love didn't exist. Frank was actually the one that brought it to my attention years ago. I mean it made perfectly good sense because of the line of work I was in. I mean who could really fall in love with a passion for killing. I been done killed a nigga over leaving the toilet seat up. After Cellus I pretty much gave up on the love thing anyway.

"Come on, ma." Sin nudged my arm and brought me from my thoughts. I walked over to the mirror and ran my fingers through my curls and then applied my lip gloss.

"Where are we going?" I asked as he appeared behind me in my reflection.

"To the hood. You ready for this?"

"The hood?" I turned around puzzled.

"Not really the hood. But my boy and his wife are having a block party. I wanted you to come."

"Ohh…" I replied, unsure about being around a crowd with him. I knew if I said no he would throw a fit so I was game.

"Why yo ass always got on black like somebody died?" Sin asked, looking over my clothing.

"Why? You don't like my outfit?" I turned to face him.

"Hell yeah it's sexy; I just noticed you always wear black." Him telling me this let me know he was paying close attention to me.

I looked at my shirt and brushed it down in the front as I bit into my bottom lip. I was so damn embarrassed I made a mental note about this.

As Sin and I walked to his car, he grabbed my hand like he always did. I noticed he was beginning to make that a habit. No matter where we went, or where we were, he always showed affection. It was really flattering but due to circumstances it kinda bothered me. We climbed into his car and pulled out of the lot and straight to the highway. Just before we got on, Sin dropped his top and my hair instantly began to blow in the wind. The sun was out and for it to have been fall, it was a nice warm day.

Yeah, you gon' fall through every time a nigga call you
That's why I ball how I ball when I spoil you
We was in Miami, first time I saw you
I was in a Phantom when I pulled up on you

As the music spilled from the speakers, I looked over from time to time and Sincere was so in tune with the song. I could tell he liked it because I've heard him play it quite a few times. Each time he rapped along he would look over at me and squeeze my hand tighter, just like now. Our entire drive he made sure to keep my hand wrapped into his all the way until we pulled up to cookout.

As we drove through the crowd of people, I caught the desirous glares from women that crowded the streets. Men aligned the streets chanting Sin's name as if he was some type of God. Moving along, Sin ignored his surroundings as if he was used to it. He pulled into an empty spot then motioned for me to exit the car. When we stepped out, my body tensed up instantly.

"Stop fidgeting, ma," he told me and pulled me into him. He wrapped his arms around my neck and stood behind me as he guided me towards the party. On the way, Sin talked to a few guys and let me go so he could shake hands with a few. I waited to the side and pretended I was busy on my phone. Once he was done, he pulled me over towards a huge tent and then stepped off to talk to a guy accompanied by a lady.

"Sin...my boy." The man stood from the chair and gave Sin a hug.

"Sup, my nigga? How you doing, Tiff?" Sin waved to the lady.

"Boy, don't wave at me; you better give me a hug." She smiled and walked over to hug him.

"Tiff, this my girl, Queen; Queen, this Tiff, the lady of the party."

"How are you doing, Queen?" She extended her hand and smiled as we shook. She seemed very polite and instantly I got a great vibe from her.

"Y'all want something to eat?" the guy asked.

"No, I'll take something to drink," I replied, thirsty as hell.

"What do you want, Queen? Soda or Hennessy?" the lady asked, making me laugh.

"Um, I'll take Hennessy." I looked at Sin and he shrugged his shoulders. The lady scurried off to get my drink and the guy invited me to have a seat. Just as I took my seat, Sin told me he would be right back. I watched him as he strolled coolly over to a crowd of men. They all started dabbing him up as if they hadn't seen him in a while. I sat back, watching him and it amazed me how much love he got from the world. Because I was so private and had been for years these types of things were extraordinary. This man was like a monarch. His stature was of one as well. Whenever I pictured a man fit to be a king, I pictured him muscular with long locs like a God. Sincere fit the exact description from his hair down to the athletic legs he possessed.

"Here you go, Queen." Tiff had come back with my drink and she took a seat beside me. We instantly began talking and before I knew it, I was tipsy and had begun to enjoy myself. She asked me questions of how I met Sin and I didn't know what the hell to say. I made up some shit about driving down New York Ave and I had a flat tire. She really wasn't prying just trying to make small talk. From time to time we would laugh about everything going on around us. Next thing I knew, two hours had passed and I drank

three cups. It was crazy because I had begun to miss Sin. Therefore, I exchanged numbers with Tiff although I would never call
her.

I stood to my feet and walked outside of the tent and began
to scan the crowd. When my eyes landed on him, he was standing
near a motorcycle and again he had a crowd around him. There
were two girls that stood close to him and whatever he was saying had them giggling. I don't know why, but I got slightly jealous just watching him entertain them. I guess he could feel I was
watching him because he looked over in my direction and we
locked eyes. That sexy ass smile he always hit me with graced his
face and then he motioned for me to come to him.

Although Sin didn't care for my black, I knew I was looking
good so I put on my sexiest walk and headed over to him. I was
wearing a black biker jacket, a black BeBe halter top that exposed
my stomach and a pair of hip hugging cotton shorts that show-
cased every curve I had. On my feet were a pair of DK peep-toe
pumps with a chrome heel to match the zippers on my jacket.
Since I'd been around Sin I had been pulling out my good clothing.
Normally I was in sweats because I stayed cooped up in my home.
Either that or I was in a trench coat on my way to seduce John.

"What's up, baby girl, you enjoying yourself?" Sin asked, pulling me in. Before answering him, I caught the envious glares of the
girls who stood to his left side.

"Yes, babe, Tiff is so nice." I called him that on purpose. And
just like I figured one girl turned her nose up.

"Yeah, her and Ron cool people."

"Shoot, Sin." A younger guy walked up shaking a pair of dice
and Sin began laughing.

"Little nigga, I'll take all yo money and you gone be crying to
yo granny." Sin chuckled and looked over towards the tent. "Tiff,
come get yo grandson before I break his little ass?" he called out.

"Grandson?" I looked at Sin then to the young boy. Tiff didn't
look a day over thirty although I could tell she was older by the
way she spoke.

"Take his money that's on his ass." Tiff waved them off. The young guy pulled out a wad of money and waved it into Sin's face.

"Man, what yo little bad ass doing with all that bread? Let me find out you out here doing some illegal shit Ima beat yo ass," Sin told him on a more serious note.

"I'm good, Sincere," was all he said and I saw right through him. He was indeed doing something he had no business but it was cute how Sin appeared to care.

"Come on, man." Sin pulled his money from his pocket and kneeled down. He and the young guy both dropped their money and began shooting. I watched from the side line trying to figure out the game. I mean I had shot craps in the casino so I assumed they were not much different. I wanted so badly to place a bet on the young man because everytime he rolled he hit a seven. Like I said, I was buzzing and had loosened up.

Twelve

Sincere

"Bet I hit six, eight?"

"Bet you won't hit a straight six?"

"Bet." I dropped my bread. This little nigga, Chris, was trying to play me in front of Queen. He had been hitting my ass since we been shooting and each time he looked over at her making her laugh.

"Let me get a bet." This guy nigga name of Steel walked up with his money in hand. Before I knew it, we had a crowd around us and it began to grow over the minutes. From time to time, I looked at Queen and she was smiling. I could tell her ass was drunk and I knew it was gonna happen because both Tiff and Ron got fucked up on a regular.

I had been knowing Tiff and Ron for years and they were like family. Once I got in the game I was on a rise so I was always too busy to attend their events but I tried to make everyone I could. Ron didn't fuck around in the streets and Tiff owned a hair salon in Manhattan. They were very family-oriented and had great vibes.

"Sincere, telephone." I heard Tiff call my name. The way she was looking, I knew it couldn't have been anybody but Helen. *Damn,* I cursed myself because it was my roll. Standing to my feet,

I placed my bread in Queen's hand and told her to roll for me. *Yeah, her ass drunk,* I thought because she had loosened up a whole lot. She took the dice eagerly and kneeled down to begin shooting. Shaking my head, I walked over to Tiff and took the phone from her hand.

"Yeah?"

"I've been calling you," Helen spoke into the phone.

"My bad, I've been shooting dice."

"Shooting dice?" I could hear the frown on her face. Helen hated when I indulged in any hood activities and it's crazy because when she met me I was on some hood shit daily. Just because I moved plenty of weight, and didn't hang out much, my lifestyle wasn't gonna change.

"Man, what's up?" I asked her in annoyance. Lately, it's like everything she said or did has begun to annoy me. At home she nagged and I would just leave. I knew it had a lot to do with Queen because everyday a nigga was falling for her more. I wanted to be in her presence 24/7 so when I was at home with Helen I'd get frustrated. Queen and I had been kicking it heavy for the last few weeks and a nigga was beginning to get accustomed to her presence.

"So I guess you just forgot about me. You didn't even ask if I wanted to come to the cookout. I'm tired of sitting in this house."

"Helen, anytime I ask you if you wanna go somewhere you say no. And why would I wanna bring you with me if all you gon' do is criticize what I'm doing?"

"I'm not criticizing anything. I just…"

"Man, I'll be there in a few hours." I cut her short.

"Okay," she spoke sadly and then got silent. I knew right then I was beginning to fuck up. I hung the phone up and Tiff was all in my grill. I handed her her phone and shook my head because I saw it coming.

"You like this chick, huh?" she asked as she flicked the ashes from her cigarette.

"You know I can't lie to you Tiff, hell yeah I do."

"I could tell. Hell, you ain't never brought a chick around.

Shit, I didn't even think yo ass was a cheater," she said and began chuckling.

"I'm not. I just got caught up," I spoke attentively. "This chick down to earth and got a dope ass vibe." I looked in Queen's direction. She was still bent down shooting and just her huge smile did something to a nigga.

"Just be careful, Sin. Don't fuck up yo whole life for one night. You and Helen have been together for awhile. Now I'm not telling you don't be happy, I'm just telling you to think rationally. I see that gleam in your eyes. She does seem like a sweet girl," Tiff added as we both looked in Queen's direction. "Why the hell you ain't bring your mother?" Tiff changed the subject.

"She will kill me if she finds out." I shook my head remembering I didn't tell my mom about the cookout.

"I won't tell if..." Tiff went to say but the sound of comotion made us both look over. Queen was now standing and Steel was in her face talking shit.

"Hold up," I told Tiff and then headed over to the dice game.

"Bitch, I hit my muthafucking point!" Steel shot at Queen. My blood instantly began to boil hearing him call her a bitch.

"I ain't gonna be another one of your bitches!" Queen stood her ground.

"Bitch, you gone..." Steel went to say but didn't get a chance. Queen did some crazy shit locking his arms through hers. She spun around with his back to hers and flipped him. The shit happened so fast I didn't get a chance to make it over in time.

"Like I said I ain't gone be another one of your bitches." She had her heel etched in his neck like it was a blade. I kneeled down into Steel's face, and put my pistol in his mouth. I wanted so badly to blow this nigga wig back but I couldn't. I wouldn't disrespect Tiff and all the kids that had stopped to see what was going on.

"Now, I should let her slit yo fucking throat but because you're Ron's nephew, Imma let you live. When you get up off this ground, you're gonna kiss her muthafucking feet and apologize. Now are we clear?" His eyes widened and he shook his head yes. Queen still had her foot in the nigga's neck and I could tell she didn't wanna let him up. Seconds later, she let him up with ease but continued to watch him through a pair of cold ass eyes. Steel lifted from the ground and began apologizing.

"Kiss her fucking feet." I went to reach for my strap again and he did as told. Since he wanted to be so bold and disrespect her, then I was gonna embarrass his ass.

"That's what yo ass get for always disrespecting someone. You know damn well Sin don't play dumb ass boy." Ron came over, shaking his head. "I apologize, Miss." Ron looked over to Queen. She nodded her head but she had this crazy ass look on her face. *Yeah, it's time to roll,* I thought, not taking my eyes off of her. She looked like she was ready to finish the nigga off. Just thinking 'bout the way she handled him, I tried not to laugh in his face.

"It was nice meeting you, Tiff." Queen looked over in Tiff's direction. I shook my head and chuckled. I gave Tiff a hug and then Ron, and with that, we left the event.

"Man, where the fuck you learn this shit? I'm starting to think you are a part of some kind of mob." I chuckled, looking over at Queen. We had just pulled up to the room where her car was parked. I wanted so badly to go inside and snatch her clothing off her and fuck the life out her sexy ass but after talking to Helen I decided to head home.

"I took self defense when I was a kid." She smirked, followed by a giggle.

"Yeah, okay." I hit her with a smirk. "Come here, let me get a kiss."

She reached over and kissed me. She then took me by surprise when she grabbed my head and went deeper into the kiss. When she pulled back, she dropped her head and smiled bashfully.

"I'll see you later." I brushed my hand across her leg.

"You're leaving?"

"Yeah, I gotta handle some shit."

"Oh okay," she replied, sounding kinda down I was shaking.

"Ima come scoop you tomorrow, I got something special lined up for you."

"Okay." She faintly smiled.

"If you want we can just chill at yo crib tomorrow."

"Or we could just chill at yours."

"Ha ha ha, we can but in my crib you gone be taking that shit off."

"Let's do it." She smirked again and then chuckled.

"Yeah, aight, baby girl. I'll see you tomorrow."

"Okay." She opened her door and hopped out.

"Q Bee," I called out to her and she turned around. "I miss you, ma."

She smiled so damn sexy I wanted to say fuck Helen and fuck home period. Damn, this girl was doing something to me. I threw my whip in reverse and backed out the lot. I stopped at the exit and waited for her to pull off. When she swooped behind me, I made my right turn and she made her left. Going home was gonna be hard because I knew I was gonna start missing her. I was missing her already and we were only apart for a few minutes.

Thirteen

John

"Honey, where did this come from?"

I turned around and Kathryn was holding a silver heart locket necklace. Instantly I became nervous because I knew exactly where it had come from. *Queen*. It was the necklace that she always wore so the last time I saw her she had to have snagged it when she quickly hid inside the closet.

"Umm...I brought it for Megan but after getting it appraised I found out it wasn't real. I'm gonna take it back," I lied. She walked over to me and placed the necklace into my hand.

"Oh okay. It's really pretty." She smiled and headed out the door. Letting out a sigh, I opened the locket the moment she left the room. Inside was a picture of a man and a woman who I assumed were Queen's parents. She resembled the man a lot but she was a split image of the woman. I stared at the locket for a brief moment and then closed it into the palm of my hand. I was gonna keep it because this was the only thing I had to remind me of the Queen. Well, except the sweet memories of our love affair.

Queen and I had been sneaking around for a while now and I found myself suddenly in love. I didn't know anything about her except her name finally. The first day she came to my home is still unknown but the way she seduced me left no room for worrying why this strange lady came into my home, put a pistol in my mouth and tied me up. I was still scared to death but after the way she made love to my shaft with the warmness of her mouth I fell into a trance. After a blissful moment of Queen bringing me to my peak, she seductively kissed my forehead and just like that, she vanished. I quickly jumped up and headed over to the window but there was not one trace of her. It's like she vanished into thin air. I closed my eyes and told myself to wake up from the dream but I wasn't dreaming.

Two weeks later she climbed through my bedroom window and this time we made love. After that, it had become a routine that felt unreal. Queen was like a fantasy. I thought of her all day everyday, nearly losing my mind. It was crazy because she had always come while Kathryn was at work like she knew my wife's schedule, which was crazy. Every night I laid in my bed craving just the scent of her. I had become so addicted to her that when I made love to my wife, I'd envision it was Queen instead.

For the last few weeks, I hadn't seen her and it was driving me crazy. Something in my heart told me that she was satisfying someone else the way she had been doing me. And each thought, I cried myself to bed. I was falling madly in love with a woman I didn't know. I didn't know where to find her. I didn't know what kind of car she drove. All I had was the name *Queen* and her fragrance *Christian Dior Poison*. For nights, I've searched every Queen in New York but none appeared to be her. For days I sat in my windowpane praying that she would come but there was not one sign of her.

My wife constantly asked was I okay and each time I lied. I wasn't okay, I was dying inside slowly. I wanted so bad to wrap her in my arms and tell her how much I loved her. I loved my wife but she was no Queen. This chick had me ready to give it all up to be with her. I wanted more than just some strange affair that took place seldomly. I wanted her to become the woman I went to sleep with every night. I wanted Queen and Queen only.

Sincere

"So you're leaving again?"

"I got shit to handle, Helen."

"Like what? Sincere, when have you left this house like this? You leave everyday, early in the morning then wonder yo ass in here in the middle of the night. If I didn't know any better, I'd think you had someone else."

"So now I got a curfew?" I looked up from the bed. I wasn't gonna answer the question about somebody else because the shit was true.

"Is there someone else?!" Helen screamed out, looking at me like she was ready to cry.

"Have I ever given you any reason to think I was cheating on you?" I stood to my feet and fixed the cuff in my pants. I was trying hard not to look her in the eyes because lying is one thing I hated.

"No, you haven't but you never stayed out like this."

"Well, I'm just handling business, baby." I walked over to her and kissed her forehead. She didn't say another word but knowing how women were, her ass was gonna start investigating. I was ten steps ahead of Helen so any traces of me and Queen had been erased. I knew her number by heart and since she didn't have any social media I really didn't have to worry. I swear Queen was a different kind of woman. These millenium bitches craved social media. With Queen, that shit didn't fascinate her. She told me how other than work, she enjoyed reading. It really didn't take me by surprise because she looked like the type of chick that would curl up on her sofa with a good book. What puzzled me though was, she mentioned work. I guess she worked on commission because anytime I called her ass she would answer. Anytime I told her to meet me she would come and this was any time any day.

Q'Bee: *Same place?*
Me: *Yep!*

I dropped my phone and pulled out the driveway of my crib. Today I was gonna take Queen to the carnival and I couldn't wait. I wanted to do something fun with her. I mean the Shakespeare play was hella cool but I remembered her mentioning she loved roller coasters. Me myself, I hated rides. I hated the way my stomach dropped and not to mention anything could happen while in the air. So guess what, her ass could have that shit. I was gonna be on the sideline snapping pictures.

When I pulled up to our normal meeting spot, Queen was sitting in her whip with the mirror down, applying her gloss. When she saw me pull in, she looked over and smiled. She quickly closed the mirror and began packing her things in her purse. She then climbed out and headed for my car. As her hips swayed in a little ass skirt, I couldn't help to notice she was wearing all white. I thought about the day I mentioned she always wore black so I guess she thought I didn't like it. I didn't mean to offend her. I just asked a question because she always wore black. Queen was a different breed of women. Other than the black, she knew how to shoot a gun and damn sure defend herself. It was crazy because her conversation was always shy but bubbly with a pinch of sex appeal that made a nigga ready to leave home. It had gotten to the point where my wife saw the signs and if Helen saw it, shit was bad. I never felt like this over a woman, and something told me in weeks to come, shit was only gonna get worse.

Fourteen

Queen

Pulling up to the NY carnival my eyes beamed looking over the bright lights and the huge Ferris wheel that lit up the entire sky. I looked over to Sincere and once again this guy amazed me. Just like I said when he took me to the play, I would never take him for a guy that loved doing romantic things. Although a fair wasn't much, it was the thought that counted. Sincere was a well paid man and with wealth came business. However, he always made time for me. Sincere could have been anywhere across the world but instead we were spending time at a carnival. I couldn't wait until he won me a stuffed animal. I know this sounds crazy but after my job was done, I would keep it for memories.

As Sin and I headed into the carnival, he grabbed my hand and led me over to the cotton candy machine. He purchased me a pink one and took a bite out of it before he passed it to me.

"Let's get on the spaceship."

"Hell no, ma."

"Come oooon, I know you didn't come here to not ride anything."

"I don't fuck with rides. Man, anything can happen up there," he said and looked up just as the roller coaster came flying through the sky.

"You trust me, right?" I tugged at his arm. I couldn't believe I said it but I knew it was the only thing that may have worked.

"Yeah, I trust *you*; it's them screws and shit I don't trust." He shook his head, looking around at all the rides. I shot him my little puppy eyes he loved so much and all he could do was shake his head. "Come on, girl. One ride so you better pick the best one." I pulled him in the direction of the spaceship. The entire time I was smiling and Sin tried hard not to laugh. When I finally broke him, he looked excited, until the ship began to spin. He latched onto the straps and his eyes nearly popped out of his head. "Ima kill you, Queen!" was all I heard before the ride began to spin faster.

After Sin and I rode our first ride, I convinced him to get on more. I saved the dragon for last and he wasn't too pleased with that ride.

"Okay, the roller coaster doesn't make your stomach drop. Let's go." I pulled his arm and led him to the line.

"Man, this line is long. Come on," he said and pulled my arm. I looked at him like he was crazy. We bypassed all the people and when we got two people from the front a little boy that stood with his mother looked up and frowned.

"Heeey, no cutting," the Caucasian boy said to Sin. We both began to laugh except the boy and his mother.

"Here, little man," Sin said and handed the boy a fifty. He used both hands to look over the bill and then looked up to Sin with a huge smile.

"Ladies first." He motioned with his hand for me to step in front of him. I couldn't help but burst out into laughter. And just like I thought, his mother was smiling now. It was crazy how money ruled the world.

When the ride stopped we waited for the patrons to exit out the side gate and then were let on.

"Man, this shit bet not break down while I'm in the air." Sin buckled his belt and laid his head back. Just as I went to say something, the coaster began to take off. I looked over at Sin and he looked calm until...*swooosh*! We went down in full speed.

The entire time on the roller coaster, I was laughing hard as hell. My hair was blowing in the window and I held my arms in the air. Finally Sin began to laugh along and I was happy because he wasn't feeling the dragon ride for shit. I was happy he had opened up because coming to a carnival and not riding rides was boring.

As soon as we got off the ride, Sin looked down at his watch. It was nearly midnight and the clouds began to form gray. Every now and then I looked up and I knew it was gonna rain at any moment but that was another thing I loved. I loved the rain and in rainy weather was when I had my most satisfying hits.

"Hold up, ma," Sin said and walked over to a shooting game.

"You knock out the complete star, you win that," the man said and pointed up to a huge unicorn stuffed animal.

"Easy," Sin said and grabbed the bebe gun. He looked into the scope and took his time to focus in.

Tat tat tat tat tat Tat tat tat tat tat Tat tat tat tat tat
Tat tat tat tat tat Tat tat tat tat tat Tat tat tat tat tat
Tat tat tat tat tat Tat tat tat tat tat

He shot until the gun began to click. He sat it down just as the man used the string to pull it towards us.

"We have a winner!" the man shouted and began ringing a bell.

"Yaaay!" I jumped up and down and excited to receive my teddy.

"I told you I got this, baby." He kissed my cheek and handed me the stuffed animal.

"Thank you." I kissed him back and hugged the bear into my arm. It was so huge I was happy we would be leaving soon because I couldn't imagine walking around the entire carnival with this thing. "Let's get on the Ferris wheel. Last ride because it's gonna rain any minute."

"Yeah and yo ass got on that short ass skirt," he added, looking over my outfit. "Hell yeah I'm with the Ferris wheel."

"I bet yo scary ass is." I playfully punched him.

When we got to the Ferris wheel, the line was short because

of the time so we were quickly let on. As it began to go in circles, I took in the breathtaking scenery. We had a view of the skyline and the Statue of Liberty. I instantly fell into a daze just thinking about how much fun I was having with Sincere. Then the thought of me having to kill him invaded my mind and it made me feel slightly saddened. I haven't had this much fun since Cellus. I thought about how Cellus romanced me just like Sin when we first met. Even until the day he died, he showered me with love and made me feel like a high school girl. Those same feelings had come back with Sincere. I began to think about why the mayor would want Sin dead because he didn't seem too bad. I mean I understood the game when it came to drugs and power, but Sin was so humble and generous he didn't strike me as a bad guy that someone would want to murder.

"Where are your parents?" Sincere asked, taking me by surprise. I closed my eyes for a brief moment then turned to face him. My first thought was to lie but because I had to gain his trust I figured I'd be honest. Well, slightly honest.

"My parents were murdered when I was 14," I replied and kept my head straight. I could feel Sin's eyes on me and I could tell he was blown back by my reply. "My mother was the sweetest person on earth." I smiled, thinking about my mother. She had a heart of gold and pleasantly mannered. I remembered her always coming home complaining about her job because just like me, she had to kill people to protect herself. "My dad too, he treated me like a princess. However, they worked so much I barely saw them. I guess that's why I'm so independent and nonchalant. I really didn't have friends but one. I spent most of my time locked in my room reading. I was fascinated with reading because it gave my mind the stability I needed. Reading for me was a therapy. I remembered my mom always complaining because all I did was bury myself in a good book. I mean, she had to understand she was never there and reading was all I had to do. I guess because when she was finally home she'd want to spend time with me but I was so caught up in a bestseller I ignored her.

"Damn, that's deep, yo. So why were they killed if you don't mind me asking?"

"No, it's okay." I slightly smiled. "Coming home from work one day and someone tried to rob them. I spoke to my father the minute it happened and we talked until he took his last breath," I lied. I couldn't tell this man what my parents did because their life was confidential. The real story was, they had been ambushed inside their home. When their bodies were found they were shot execution-style and both laid down on their faces. The authorities ruled it as a robbery but I knew it was more to the story.

"I'm sorry to hear that, baby." He looked out into the night air and we both went silent.

"So what about your parents?" I asked because I didn't wanna speak too much about my life. My parents' murder was too personal and I couldn't get that personal with Sin. Getting deep into my past, made me feel like I could trust you and with Sin things were different. I couldn't trust him because I couldn't trust myself. I had a job to do so how could I let my guards down enough to trust?

"My mom is around," he said and didn't bother to mention his father. If he wanted me to know then I'm sure he would volunteer the information.

"So when Ima meet my mother-in-law?" I asked, nudging his arm.

"After I hit that pussy. If you're welcomed into my family, I gotta know if the pussy good first," he chuckled, making me laugh.

"I guess me and moms won't ever meet." I smirked, making him laugh out loud.

"You still scared of me, Queen?" he asked but this time he wasn't smiling. I looked out into the air and then back to Sincere.

"I'm scared of myself, Sincere. Love doesn't exist in my world," I told him as a sharp pain shot through my body. Just looking at Sin I wanted so badly to cry. He would never understand me and the shit hurt. It wasn't really just about Sin, it was any man. A man in my life meant, meet, have sex, fall in love then move in and have some babies. What man in their right mind would agree to dating a damn hitman? I mean, I thought of leaving the game but I was too accustomed to it. Not only did I get paid great, but I had become fascinated with killing.

"No matter how much money in the world you have, love is the only thing that would keep you grounded. You gotta find happiness one day, ma," he said, just as the ride stopped.

I looked at Sin in his eyes and then reluctantly replied, "Love doesn't exist in my world, Sincere."

Fifteen

Sincere

Walking towards the car, I couldn't get the conversation with Queen out of my head. I found it odd that not only her boyfriend but her parents were also murdered on some wrong place wrong time type of shit. I could tell that those incidents scorned her heart and she was in a shell. When she said love didn't exist, that shit blew me back. I wanted so badly to tell her it did and even tell her I'd make her love me, but how could I when I was already spoken for? The shit made me feel guilty. As badly as I wanted to, I couldn't promise Queen my heart. I could give her the world and everything she deserved but she was worth more than some side chick type shit. Baby girl was wife material and it hurt to say, that one day she was gonna make some nigga a happy man.

As we walked through the carnival, I looked up in the sky and the clouds had begun to form a really dark grey color. Queen said it was gonna rain but I didn't wanna believe it until now. Suddenly I felt a drop hit the side of my face, so I grabbed the unicorn I had won for her so we could hurry to the car. By the time we made it, it had begun to shower and I knew it would storm soon.

"Nice unicorn," I heard a voice behind us and looked to see where it had come from. *Shit,* I thought as my eyes fell onto my wife. She had her arms crossed over one another as she stared me coldly in the eyes. Her eyes then shifted from me to Queen and by Queen's pause of reaction, I knew she was wondering who this woman could be.

"Man, Helen, take yo ass home," I said in hopes she would just listen. But nah, her foul ass mouth just had to say some slick shit.

"May I ask who you are? I'm Helen, Sincere's wife," she said and flashed her ring. Queen's eyes bulged as she looked from Helen to me.

"I'm Queen, the bitch that's not to be fucked with. And if you're here to start trouble, believe me you don't want these problems. Now I don't know what you and this man..." Queen used her hand to point in my direction. "...has going on, but I had no idea he was married."

"Trust me, I'm not worried about your little threats. And nigga, don't get quiet now. You parade around town with a bitch winning bears and shit while your wife is at home."

"Bitch?" Queen shot and then tried to walk over to Helen. I quickly grabbed her arm and pulled her behind me.

"Helen, take yo ass home. We will talk about this when I get there."

"I'm not going anywhere without you. You think you're about to just leave with her?"

"Man, take yo muthafucking ass to the crib before you make me do some shit Imma regret."

"Wow, so this what it is? You get caught and now you threaten to do something to me," Helen's voice began to crack.

"Man, because yo ass ain't listening to me." I turned from Helen to Queen. "Get in the car, Queen." I opened Queen's door but she didn't move. She looked Helen in the eyes and I could tell Helen's tears were getting to her. Her face slightly softened as she continued to stare.

"Man, get yo ass in the car," I told her and shoved her into the car. I slammed her door shut and then turned to face Helen.

"I'll just pack my things and go. 'Cause whoever this chick is, got you open."

"Man, yo ass ain't going nowhere! You better be there when I get there." I turned to walk away from her. I climbed into the driver's seat and before I pulled off I looked at Helen. She was still standing there and I could tell she was crying. Her tears had blended with the rain but it was evident she was hurt because of the frown on her face. Our eyes connected and I let out a deep sigh. Like I stated before I had never stepped out on my wife so a nigga was feeling fucked up.

As Queen and I drove towards her car, the ride was silent. The only sounds that could be heard were from the heavy rain and windshield wipers that swooshed from side to side. Queen looked out the window and I could tell she was disappointed. I wanted so badly to speak but what could a nigga really say? I was caught shit. However, I had to make this shit right. I couldn't let Queen get out of my car mad at me. I was scared I would never see her again.

"You mad at me?" I asked, looking in her direction. She continued to look out the window and remained silent. "Man, I didn't mean for this shit to happen. Trust me, this has never happened before."

"Yeah, I bet." She rolled her eyes.

"Real shit, a nigga don't just be out here fucking all types of bitches. I love my wife."

"Well, if you love her so much, stay the fuck away from me," she said and reached for the door handle.

"What the fuck you doing, yo?"

"Sincere, just leave me the fuck alone. I'm getting out right here and you don't have to worry about me."

"Yo ass ain't getting out shit. It's late as fuck and we in the middle of nowhere. Ima take you where the fuck I picked you up from."

"I swear on my mama if you don't let me out, Ima jump out this muthafucka. And trust me, I'll land on my feet. I've done it plenty of times." My head shot over in her direction and with the shit Queen was doing, I found this statement to be true. Nothing with this chick would surprise me.

I pulled my car to the side of the road and she quickly jumped out. She didn't try to cover her hair like most girls did when they had a fresh hairdo. The rain was falling down hard and instantly she was drenched. I quickly jumped out and caught up to her. I tugged at her arm and pulled her back towards the car.

"Just leave me the fuck alone."

"That's the problem, I ain't never leaving you alone." I looked her in the face seriously. She needed to understand it. And especially after getting caught, my wife was prolly gone leave a nigga and hell nah, I wasn't gonna be on the losing end.

"You crazy in yo fucking head if you think Ima ever play side bitch to a nigga. I can have plenty niggas, Sin, and not to mention my pussy too fucking good for that," she shot as the rain fell down into her face.

Just looking at her and the way her face frowned made me forget all about Helen who was at home crying her eyes out. At this point nothing mattered but Queen. Her hair was now soaking wet and I could see her hardened nipples through her white shirt. It was evident she wasn't wearing a bra and the way she was looking had a nigga dick hard.

"Real shit, Queen, I had never even cheated on my wife. I love the fuck out of her."

"This the second time you said it, so if you love her so much, then why you fucking with me?"

"Because a nigga falling for you. There, I said it! What, you want me to tell the world?" I turned around with my hands wide. "I want the world to know I love the fuck out this chick right here. Anybody, somebody that hears this shit, I love Queen!" my voice echoed in the night's air. I turned back around to face her again. She was looking at me like I was crazy but this shit was real. Every day spent with Queen was making me fall for her more and more. Shit was to the point that when I fucked my wife, I pictured Queen. I couldn't even focus on shit else in life because she crossed my mind frequently.

"Love doesn't exist in my world," she said softly and I could tell she believed that bullshit.

"Let me love you and I promise I'll figure this shit out." I stepped up on her so close I could feel the heavy breathing that seeped from her lips. Unintentionally, I kissed her. When she tried to pull back, I grabbed her head and forced her to kiss me.

Before I knew it, we were having a full blown make out session in the rain. The more we kissed, the more shit got heated. I picked Queen up into my arms, never breaking our kiss. I walked her over to the hood of my car and sat her down. Without warning, I slid my hands in between her thighs and pulled her panties to the side. I began playing with her pussy and she broke our kiss to let out a sexy ass moan that made my dick so hard I couldn't take it. That gave me the invitation to slide her panties off and then release my dick from my pants.

The entire time, we both looked each other in the eyes. Our stare down was so damn intimate fire burned between us. I cocked her legs open and then slid her down to me. Thanks to the rain her pussy was extra wet so I slid my dick into her. She let out a moan followed by a gasp that told me I felt good inside of her. As I began to pump in and out of her, her mouth fell open and she started panting my name. I bit into my bottom lip because this girl's pussy was hugging my dick for dear life. *Damn, she wasn't lying. Her pussy good as fuck*, I thought, watching her sexy ass facial expressions.

"Q Bee, look at me, ma," I demanded because she had closed her eyes to break our stare down. When she looked at me, I began hitting her pussy walls with long nice strokes. "I ain't never letting you go. I can't let you go, ma." I was talking not only to her but to her pussy. "You hear me, Queen?" When she didn't respond, I started plunging harder inside of her.

"Yes, Sin...oh, my Gooood...yessss, I hear you. Shit, I hear you." Her legs began to shake, making it hard for her to talk.

"That's right. Cum for me, baby." I could feel her juices melting onto my dick. I made her cum long and hard but made sure to slow down so I didn't bust prematurely.

As Queen and I continued to make love in the rain, I had forgotten about everything in my life. Her pussy was so tranquilizing that I wanted to stay here forever. However, knowing that someone could possibly see us, I began to focus on my nut. "Shiiit!" I shouted, not being able to help it.

I released every drop into her and then fell on top of her. I was breathing hard and I could feel her heart thump in her chest. When I finally pulled back to look at her, a trace of tears was on her face. Her eyes were now closed so I bent down to kiss her tears away. Suddenly her eyes shot open and she gave me a look I couldn't read. Something about the look wasn't sitting right with me. I pulled out of her and she slid off the car. I fixed myself and then went to grab something so she could clean up with and when I turned back around she was nowhere in sight.

I began scanning my surroundings but it's like she vanished. My eyes fell down to her panties that laid in a puddle of water so I grabbed them and stuck them in my pocket. I let out a deep sigh and shook my head. I got so lost into my thoughts, I didn't realize I was leaning on my whip, in the rain, hoping she would appear. I ended up staying there until I finally realized she was gone.

Sixteen

Queen

A few weeks later...

Am I Queen of Fools?
Wrapped up in lies and foolish jewels
What do I see in you?
Maybe I'm addicted to all the things you do
'Cause I keep thinking you were
The one who came to take claim of this heart
Cold-hearted shame you'll remain just afraid in the dark

I fell into a trance listening to Nicki Minaj's "Grand Piano." The song was a perfect fit for what I was going through with Sincere. I felt like I had been played like a grand piano and although this love was a setup, I found myself feeling despair. It had been weeks since we talked and trust me everyday that went by I thought of him. I had Franko on my ass now about the hit and he kept saying it was almost time. Each time he mentioned it, I brushed him off by saying I needed more time.

The night I vanished from Sincere, I went home and broke down. I cried for so many hours that I never realized I was sitting on my living room floor. My emotions were all over the place. The memory of our sex escapade played in my mind and the thoughts were bittersweet. The scenery was so perfect, his sex was so perfect—actually too damn perfect—that it only confused my heart more. Him being married was only gonna make it easier for me to kill him, but now, after that session I was off balance. He had been calling me nonstop but I needed to get over this man before I gave in. As much as I tried to front, I was falling for him too. However, I used him having a wife to ease my mind and continue with my plan.

"Reina! Oh my God, heeeey," a woman's voice broke me from my daze. I looked into John's face before I turned to see who had called me by my government name.

"Rihanna? Oh my Gooood...it's been years." I stood from my chair and wrapped my arms around her. I hadn't seen my best friend in nearly ten years.

"How's everything going? Girl, give me your number. We got some catching up to do." She smiled, happy to see me.

"Great. I've been just great." I peered down to John who was all in our mouths.

After a week of crying over Sin, I finally went to see John. Somehow I let him convince me into going out and guess where we ended up? Piccola.

"I'm gonna call you, love."

"Okay. It was nice seeing you, bestie." I smiled and we hugged again. The minute I took my seat, John looked at me and asked exactly what I knew he would.

"Reina?"

"It means Queen in Spanish," I quickly replied. "So how did you manage to get out of the house?" I changed the subject.

"Queen, you know how. Hell, you know everything about my life."

"She's at work." He nodded *yes*.

"So where have you been? I've been missing you, Queen." He looked at me with pleading eyes.

"I've been working, John."

"Doing?" he asked, just as my phone began to ring. When I

pulled it from my bag, I assumed it was Sin who I was gonna send to voicemail like always. When I looked at the screen it was an unknown number.

"Excuse me, I have to take this." I stood from the table and headed outside to get some privacy.

"May I help you?"

"Oh my God, Queen," Tiff cried into the phone.

"What's wrong?" I asked because she sounded so rattled.

"Sinc...Sincere..." she broke down.

"Is Sincere okay?" I shouted into the phone.

"I don't know. He was shot and we don't know how bad it is. Ron's on his way to the hospital with Sincere's mother."

"Oh no..." my heart sank. I began walking towards the street so I could flag down a taxi. I needed to get to my car and fast.

"He's on his way to Bellevue Hospital."

"Okay. I'll be there," I replied and then disconnected the phone. I hopped into the first cab that pulled over and just as I was climbing in John stepped outside of the restaurant. As the taxi made it's U-turn, I looked at John and our eyes connected. He wore a despairing look on his face. "I'm sorry," I mouthed the words hoping he read my lips. I laid back in my seat and closed my eyes. I knew I wasn't supposed to feel like this, but this was confirmation I fell in love with Sin. Just hearing Tiff say he was shot did something to me. I said a silent prayer in hopes he pulled through.

"Queen."

"Surprised to see me?"

"How...how'd you get in my home?"

"Mayor Jones, did you forget who the fuck I was?" I asked, taking a seat across from him. He nervously looked around and I was sure he was looking for his guards.

"They're all dead," I assured him, thinking about the three guards that were laid out in his front lawn. "If you try anything,

I'm gonna pull this pin and blow us all up. I'm sure your wife and kids are sleeping peacefully." I showed him the M67 grenade I had in my hand. His eyes shot open wide and he looked like he would shit himself any minute.

"Oooh, steak," I said and reached over to grab his meat from his plate. Mayor Jones was weak as hell in my eyes but the money he paid was so good I got the job done.

"What do you want?" he finally spoke. I didn't reply right away because I was too busy chewing. Once I was done, I wiped my mouth on the napkin and through it down to the table.

"Sincere." I crossed my leg over the other.

"Sincere?" he asked puzzled.

"Yes, Sincere. You know Sincere, the man that you paid me to kill. He's currently in the hospital and I'm sure you sent your men after him."

"Queen, I know Sincere but I didn't order a hit on him," he replied calmly. Something in his eyes told me he wasn't lying. He didn't have that scared look anymore; he looked more confident.

"Frank said..."

"Queen, Franko is a damn lie. I haven't ordered a hit on that man. The last hit was on the Chinese boy. Now I don't know what's going on with Franko but something is telling me he wants that boy dead and it's personal. Now if you'll let yourself out." He stood to his feet and dismissed me. There was really nothing else to say. I nodded once and stood to my feet. I let myself out and climbed into my car. I felt bad I had caused pure chaos at the mayor's home and all for nothing. I pulled out of his driveway, with so much shit on my mind.

As I drove away from Mayor Jones's house, my thoughts were cluttered. I couldn't understand why Franko would lie about the mayor ordering the hit. If he had some personal vendetta against Sin, why wouldn't he ask for the hit himself? Something about this was fishy and I couldn't wait to speak with him. Right now I was gonna head down to the hospital and make sure Sin was okay. I knew it was a possibility that his wife would be there but it didn't matter. I needed to see him. I needed to make sure he was

okay.

Seventeen

Queen

After giving the front desk Sin's name, I was giving my pass and let upstairs to his floor. When I stepped off the elevator I read the arrow that pointed in the direction of his room. With each step I took, my heart bounced off my chest more and more. As I rounded the corner, the first person I spotted was Ron, Tiff and an older lady. Across from them sat a few men that I figured were close to Sincere. Looking towards his room door, I also noticed the same two guards that were at the restaurant with him the night we went out.

"Queen," Tiff said and jumped to her feet.

"Hey, Tiff. Is he okay?" I was anxious to know.

"Yes. I tried to call you but your phone went to voicemail. He's okay, thank God. He took a bullet to the hip. Nothing major. He was asleep from the medication but he's awake now. He's only able to have two visitors at a time so right now his mother is inside." She looked at me and the look she gave me told me the second person was his wife.

Taking it upon myself, I walked towards his room. When the guards laid eyes on me, they moved to the side and let me through. The moment I stepped into the room, the first person I laid eyes on was Helen.

"Why are you here?" She jumped to her feet. I ignored her and turned the corner to Sin's bed. He looked up at me from the Jell-O he held in his hands and I could tell he was surprised to see me.

"Queen," he called my name as if I was an illusion. I walked over to his bedside and placed a kiss on his head.

"She needs to leave." Helen walked over but she made sure to stand on the other side of his bed.

"I just wanted to make sure you were okay. I'm gonna go."

"Man, you ain't going nowhere."

"Son, what's going on? Who's this?" the older woman spoke, looking from Sin to me.

"Ma, this Queen, my friend."

"It's his little bimbo I caught him with. Now can you please ask her to leave? You are not 'bout to disrespect me."

"Man, chill the fuck out!" Sincere yelled and then growled out in pain holding his side.

"Helen, you're gonna get enough of trying to control this man. If this is his friend, I'm sure she's concerned," his mother defended.

"Mrs. Ingram, with all due respect, this is my husband and if I want her gone then she needs to leave."

"And this is my goddamn son. If he aint telling her to leave then apparently he wants her here."

They both continued to argue back and forth. Mrs. Ingram was putting her foot down and already I liked her.

"It's okay, Mrs. Ingram, I'm gonna just go. I don't wanna cause any trouble. This place is swarmed with police." I smirked at Helen.

"Man, I'm a grown ass man and Helen I keep telling you that. Queen ain't leaving this muthafucka and if you don't like it, then you could bounce."

Helen looked at him and her face sunk. I could tell she was ready to cry as she watched him with her head cocked to the side. Instead of her putting up a fight, she stormed over to a chair and took a seat. I chuckled under my breath because she refused to leave Sin alone with me. She'd rather get her feelings hurt by staying than just leaving.

"Sit down," Sin said so I walked over to take a seat. "Right here," he told me and pointed to the chair that was right on the side of his bed.

"Yes, daddy." I smirked at Sin and taunted the hell out of Helen. When I looked in her direction she smacked her lips and rolled her eyes at me.

"Son, Ima gonna get out of here. It was nice meeting you, Queen. I hope I'll see you again."

"Nice meeting you too." I smiled politely.

"Love you, ma."

"Love you too, baby. See you tomorrow." She threw her purse over her shoulder and headed for the door. She didn't bother saying anything to Helen but she did shoot her an infuriating look. After a short silence in the room, Sin finally looked over at me. We held a slight gaze and he was making me nervous. I wondered if he knew anything about his shooting. Shit was so crazy right now and especially because the hit that was originally for him turned out to be something else. I really didn't mind doing hits for Franko because he paid great, however, him lying still had me puzzled.

"What's up, Miss-M-I-A." Sin smirked. I could tell he didn't want to say much because Helen was in the room. She tried to act like she didn't pay us any mind but the way her body kept shifting in her seat I knew she was all ears.

"It's not like that, friend." I shot sarcastically and I didn't understand why. Right now it wasn't about Helen anymore, I was caught up in the rapture of the moment.

"So tell me what it's like because you disappear from a nigga for weeks?"

"It's just..uhhh." I bit my bottom lip. "It's just after that night...?" I began twirling my fingers. The sound of Helen's lip smacking grabbed both me and Sin's attention. She then stood to her feet and stormed out of the room. Her soft sniffles told me she was crying and my womanism kicked in. I began to feel bad.

"Look, Sin, I'm not trying to cause any confusion in your household. Ima just go."

"Man, what I tell you, Queen? You ain't going nowhere," he said and picked up the hospital phone. He dialed a number and moments later, he began to speak.

"Yes, I'm in room 326, I need a blanket and pillow. And turn this air down, it's cold as fuck in here." He hung up the phone and looked at me. Letting out a defeated sigh, I looked straight ahead.

"If you ever leave like that again, Imma come find you. You think this shit with me a game, Queen?" he scrutinized me. "I done dissed my fucking wife for you and keep shit real, ma, I really don't give a fuck. So you need to make up yo fucking mind. Now come lay over here with me and tell daddy all about your future plans for us." He scooted over and patted the side of the bed next to him.

I could tell by the sound in his voice he was serious so I lifted from my seat and kicked off my shoes. Moments later, the nurse came in and sat the items down. I made myself comfortable because Sin made it clear I was spending the night. This man was crazy but I swear he had a bitch woozy. Everything he did tonight to make me feel special, made this hit much harder. I was still caught up over his sex game and now this. I didn't know what the hell to do at this point but I had to figure shit out fast.

The next morning I opened my eyes and I quickly had to squinch them. The rays of the sun beamed through the window right where Sin and I were asleep. I turned to face Sin and he was already awake, watching me. He gave me a warm smile before greeting me.

"Good morning, beautiful." He kissed my forehead. My eyes danced around the room. I couldn't believe I had slept that hard.

"Morning, handsome."

"I've been waiting for you to wake up with yo snoring ass."

"I do not snore." I giggled.

"Shiiiit, you ain't had no company, I see." We both laughed.

"Anyway." I playfully rolled my eyes. "Why you waiting on

me? You missed me?"

"Yep. And I needed you to change this bandage for me."

"Okay," I replied, knowing damn well this was the nurse's job. However, I still got up and grabbed the peroxide. "Where?" I asked, pulling the cover back.

"Right here," he said and grabbed my hand. He threw his arm behind his head as I slightly lifted so I could see where the womb was. *Lord this man's dick,* I thought watching his dick lay pleasantly on his thigh.

"I don't see anything."

"Man, right here." He grabbed my hand and placed it on his dick. And that's when I realized he had only gotten shot in his side. I looked up at him and his sly grin let me know exactly what he was up to.

"Suck that muthafucka," he said, causing a waterfall between my legs. I looked him in the eyes and that same fire bounced off his eyes. I took it into my hand nervously and began to stroke it slowly, jacking him off. I was contemplating with myself. I was torn between pleasing him and being embarrassed to suck his dick. I wrapped my lips around him, instantly getting it wet. I could feel his eyes on me so I tried hard not to look at him. However, I needed to steal a glance. When I looked over, he was biting into his lip and that arm behind his head reminded me of a king. Sin looked sexy as hell even in his hospital gown and locks all over his head.

"Shiiiit, Q Bee," he hissed, grabbing my head. I relaxed my throat muscles and slid my mouth all the way down until my lips touched his sack. When I did this, he really began panting.

"Suck that muthafucka, baby. I can feel it coming."

I continued on my mission to make him cum. His words had my pussy throbbing so hard I slid my hands into my tights and began touching myself.

"Hell nah, come here," he said and pulled me back. He moved up in the bed and turned to his side giving me a good angel. I turned around doggy style and slid back onto him. My love tunnel was so damn wet, I took the pain like a G 'cause I was dying to feel him inside of me. I began throwing it back and the nigga called my name. This man's dick felt so good inside of me I was biting my lip and moaning at the same damn time. Just like last time it took me into another world. It was like Heaven along with the birds and the beautiful blue skies.

"Queen, I love you, ma," he barely whispered and he made my heart sink. I started going slow then closed my eyes so I could re-play his words over and over in my mind. I didn't bother replying but my heart cried out for him. Before I knew it, I could feel my legs began to quiver and my insides causing a tidal wave. Sincere followed suit and for the second time he exploded inside of me. His cum was nice and warm, and it felt good hitting my insides. After I made sure to get every drop of him inside of me, I lifted away and headed into the restroom to clean myself.

Once I was done, I grabbed his bed pan and filled it with warm water. I pulled the towel from the rack and grabbed the soap that the hospital provided. I walked back out and headed back over to his bedside. I began to gently wash him up and the entire time he watched me. Out of nowhere, he grabbed my arm, forcing me to stop and look over at him. But, he didn't even need to say it.

"I love you too, Sin," I spoke just above a whisper. We locked eyes as always and without words we sang to each other with our eyes. The melody went something like... *I'm dangerously in love with you.*

Eighteen

John

Another couple days...

I laid in my bed watching television as Queen rained heavy on my mind. Since the night she left me at the restaurant I had been gloomy. Although her disappearing didn't surprise me, it still shattered my heart. Our date alone was too good to be true but it was all I had besides a damn necklace. I hadn't seen her since that day and because I had no way of contacting her all I could do is wait patiently for her arrival.

"Are you okay?" my wife asked with an uneven look. I hadn't even noticed her standing there.

"I'm fine."

"No you're not. You've been going into long dazes and I've noticed you moping around the house. Is it my job because I could quit?" she asked, wearing a concerned look.

"No, no, you're fine, honey, trust me."

"Well, today I took off. We're gonna watch movies and lay around. I'm going down to make popcorn," she said and waltzed out the room. Hearing her mention she had taken off from work, I became alarmed. I was praying Queen would show, hell, I prayed everyday she would show up but not today.

Moments later, Kathryn walked in holding two soda pops, a bowl of popcorn and liquid butter. I watched her as she grabbed the television tray and sat the items down. The long gown she wore with a slight bit of her breast exposed looked really good on her. Her hair had been dyed honey blonde and she wore it pinned in a bun. Kathryn was beautiful. Every time I laid eyes on her I felt bad about my affair with Queen. I didn't think too much into it most times because Queen was like a damn fantasy. My wife was gorgeous but Queen was breathtaking. Her bad girl persona and the way she demanded sex from me was a thrill and something my wife couldn't make me feel.

"Okay, so what are we watching?" Kathryn plopped down and grabbed the remote. I stuck my hand into the popcorn bowl and just as I was gonna tell her to turn to the guide, something flashed across the television that pulled my attention.

"Wait, don't turn." I stopped her. I watched closely at the man and woman whose faces were plastered on the screen. "Babe, can you go grab some napkins and bring me a piece of bread. I'm hungry," I told her so she could take extra time heading into the bread pantry.

"Sure." She lifted up and headed out the room. The moment she left, I jumped up and grabbed the necklace that Queen had lost right here in my bedroom. I opened it and sure enough the same couple that was on the news was the same two people whose picture was inside the chain.

Today the Central Intelligence Agency held its annual Memorial Ceremony to remember, honor, and celebrate the courageous lives of CIA officers Lauren Valentina Clarke and King Darnell Clarke. As the newscaster continued, my heart cringed more and more. *Queen's parents were CIA?* Hearing their names made me jump from my seat. I ran over to my computer and began typing their names into Google.

"Sorry it took me so long. John Jr. needed help with a math problem." I spun around in my chair.

"Honey, can we watch the movie later? I have some work I need to get done."

"Oh, okay," she replied pessimistically. I could tell she was a little hurt but I had things to attend to.

"I promise we'll get together later. Just give me a couple hours." I told her and then spun around in my chair.

"Okay, I'll go busy myself with the kids," she said and closed the door to give me some privacy. I turned back around and began my research. This was a start to find out more about Queen. Something was up with her and just by the way she climbed through people's windows I was certain.

Queen

I spent every day at the hospital. Sincere was adamant about my stay so he whined every time I tried to leave. To my surprise, Helen hadn't been back so we spent those days cuddled in his twin sized hospital bed. Today was the day he was finally being released because he had finally got up to walk. He couldn't drive himself so I told him I would pick him up. While we waited on him to be discharged, I needed to make a quick run. I left the hospital and jumped on the highway to Franko's mansion. I had a lot of things to get off my chest so I needed to see him and now.

When I pulled up I was immediately let in. I headed upstairs to exactly where I knew to find Franko. He was in his office where he spent his entire life. When I opened the door, just as I figured, he was behind his desk. When he looked up from his computer he wore a look I couldn't read. I didn't get the normal introduction. Instead, he just watched me and remained silent. I took a seat and dropped my bag on the ground in front of me.

"Why did you order the hit on Sincere?" I asked, not wasting any time.

"You don't walk in my damn home questioning me, dammit."

"Why did you order the hit?" I asked again. Franko's look nor his tone didn't scare me. I knew Franko and he was a hustler. A killer was something he wasn't, which is why he hired every one to do his dirty work.

"You're off the case." He turned to look at his screen.

"Why the fuck did you order the hit, Franko?" I shot to my feet, slamming the chair into the ground.

"Why I ordered the hit is none of your damn business. You get the job and you get paid. Now it's not my business nor my fault you fell in love with this piece of shit." I shot him a look but I remained silent. "Don't look like that, my love. It's written all over your face." He shook his head. "Queen, have I not taught you anything? Love doesn't exist in your world. You know why? Because love is a distraction. Just like the last boy toy you had, what's his name? Marcellus, yeah, that's him. You foolishly fell in love and he became a goddamn distraction."

"I'm not in love with Sincere. I just needed time," I replied, ignoring his statement about Cellus. However, something about the way he mentioned Cellus ' name told me something wasn't right.

Franko reached into his desk and pulled out a stack of photos. He looked at me and then slammed them on the table.

"It sure looks like you're in love to me." I looked over the pictures of Sin and I at the carnival. There were pictures of us kissing, me holding the unicorn and even us walking onto the Ferris wheel. I looked up from the pictures and I was at a loss for words. Anyone looking at the photos could see the chemistry between Sin and I.

"I umm..." I cleared my throat. "I needed to get close to him."

"Queen, what don't you get? This man doesn't love you," he said and slammed a few more pictures down. My eyes roamed the pictures of Sincere and Helen. "He's happily married and he's no good for you. Trust me if you knew the truth about Sincere, you'd forget all about him." He turned to look at his computer dismissing me. I grabbed my purse and turned for the door. I was defeated by Franko's choice of words. He was right, love was a distraction and Sin was happily married. But damn I couldn't help how I felt.

"My men are on it. We missed the last time but we won't miss again." I turned to look at him and that was confirmation that he was the one that shot Sincere. Just as I grabbed the doorknob, he called out to me again.

"Queen!"

I turned around.

"Just stick to the white boy," he said and then excused me. I watched him pensively for a slight moment and then headed out of Franko's office.

As I climbed into my car, Franko's words played over and over in my mind. Knowing he was the one that shot Sin wasn't sitting well with me. And not to mention that statement about Cellus bemused me. My heart began to do something I couldn't describe. My emotions were boggled and I couldn't even stop the tears that began to rain down my face. All I could think about was poor Cellus. He was innocent in all this. And knowing he was murdered because of me really made my heart cry. Cellus was sweet with a future ahead of him. He wanted to build aircraft. His dreams of having children and being a family were both of our dreams. And now he was dead and all because of me. I thought back to that day and visions of him falling to the ground made me cry harder. The look on his face held so much agony and discomfort that my heart shattered right there, in that very spot and I hadn't regained myself since.

Nineteen

Queen

"Heeey." I looked over as Sin climbed into my car.

"What's up, ma, why the long face?"

"Just a lot on my mind. That's all."

"Well, I'm out, now let me take everything off your mind." He licked his lips.

I couldn't help the giggles that escaped my lips because I knew exactly what he meant. I had so much on my mind right now, I couldn't even think about the dope dick he had served me. My thoughts were at an all time high and again I was confused with *why was I here in the first place*?

"Something is up with you. Queen, it's written all over your face," he said as I drove away from the hospital.

"Sin, I'm fine, baby," I assured him but he wasn't buying it. He continued to watch me and wouldn't take his eyes off me. When he finally looked away I let out a slight sigh and focused on the road. After about twenty minutes of driving, I needed to know the details of him getting shot. I wanted to know if he had any idea who it could have been.

"Did you see who shot you?" I asked without looking in his direction.

"Shit was so fast. All I remember is a black van coming out of nowhere. I didn't even see them. Shit, I pulled my strap out and squeezed back. I killed the passenger but the driver got away. I didn't even know I was shot until I hopped in my whip and my side started burning." He looked straight ahead and fell silent. "Shit just crazy because I ain't never been tried this much. Niggas know who the fuck I am and what I'm capable of. I guess they don't watch the news," he said and then turned again to look ahead.

I knew exactly what he meant about watching the news. And just as I figured, Sin was behind the gruesome murders that had taken place. However, what he didn't know was, who was really out to kill him. I don't know why, and whatever it was, Franko made sure not to tell.

"Just be careful." I replied, shocking myself. I've never used such words but I guess I finally had a reason. A part of me wanted to confess to Sin what I did for a living but I because I had killed so many innocent people I was embarrassed. Although they were on someone else's bad guy list, they were innocent in my eyes.

"Take me to get my whip so I could follow you home."

"Sin, you cannot drive right now."

"I ain't handicap, ma. Trust me, I'm good."

"And where am I taking you to?"

"My crib."

"Your crib?" I shot in his direction. "Sin, I already feel bad about us, I'm not disrespectful like that."

"First off, you my bitch and I don't give a fuck who don't like it. And keep shit real, she ain't even there. She took her shit and moved with her moms." I looked at him again and I really felt bad.

"You don't feel bad?" I asked because this was his wife. If he did this to her and so fast then what would make me any different?

"Hell yeah I feel bad. But shit, I can't help who the heart loves. Helen's cool as fuck but she ain't shit like the first day we married. She changed a lot, Queen."

"But that doesn't give you a reason to just up and leave her."

"Shit, she left me."

"Sin!" I called out to him because this wasn't funny. I mean I understand when the love fades away it's gone but I don't want to be the cause.

"You know how you asked me my favorite food, or how you asked me about my parents, or better yet, if I have any other future plans other than selling crack? Well, Helen doesn't ask that type of shit. Don't get me wrong; I know she love a nigga but is it love or lust? Is it my money or what because that's always what it's about? I mean, she bitches and complains about me being in the streets but truthfully I understand why she don't want me out there because if something happens to me, she won't have shit."

"But how when you guys are married?"

"Prenup, baby girl." He smirked. "I was in love but I wasn't no fool," he added and looked down at his phone. The ride fell silent and I drifted into another place. Sin busied himself on his phone but from time to time he would instruct me on how to get to his house. I thought about everything he said and it kinda made sense. This man felt neglected and used at home. He came to me for a spontaneous relationship; and here I was, deceiving him. *Sigh*.

Sincere

As I followed Queen to her crib, she drove like a bat out of hell. She was dipping a brand new Pagani Zonda that had 547 horsepower and 236 MPH on the dash. Her shit was wet. Each time we came to a light, she would rev her engine like she wanted to race. Now, don't get shit fucked up, I was driving my McLaren GTR and this bitch went 60 MPH in less than 2.8 seconds. However, Queen's horsepower was shitting on me. I watched her with a huge smile, as her hair blew in the wind when she sped off. I was on her ass and the entire way we zigzagged through traffic but made sure to keep up with one another.

To my surprise, Queen agreed to let a nigga come over. I couldnt wait because I needed to feel that pussy that had me sprung, dumb and dissing the fuck out my wife. I'll be fronting if I said I didn't feel bad, but keep shit real, Helen wasn't going nowhere. I learned a long time ago she would stick around because she was too accustomed to the lifestyle I provided for her. She wasn't trying to work a day in her life and because of the prenup she would walk away with nothing. She couldn't birth my seeds so there was nothing to tie us together. But real shit, because I wasn't no fucked up nigga, I would never just leave her high and dry. I always told myself if this day came, I would bless her with an easy mill that wouldn't even affect my pockets.

When we walked into Queen's crib I immediately made myself comfortable. I limped over to her plush white couch and took a seat. Taking in her décor, I was amazed at how laid her shit was. Everything in her living room was white and it was evident no one ever visited. Queen had disappeared towards the back of the house and came back shortly wearing a pair of shorts and a white top. This was the first time I was actually able to take in her frame. Although she was short and petite, her body was stacked like she worked out. She had some nice thick thighs and a flat ass stomach that made her hips look wide. As I stared over her blemish-free body, she began to fidget.

"Yo shit fly." I told her and then focused my attention on her crib.

"Thank you." She smiled and took a seat beside me.

"Where yo TV?" I asked, noticing there wasn't a TV in sight.

"It's in my bedroom. I don't really come in here."

"Aight." I stood to my feet and she watched me the entire time. I grabbed my crutch and began my detour around her home. I was gonna take it upon myself to find her bedroom so I could get comfortable and watch TV. As I passed through her dining area, I noticed a bookshelf that held tons of books. My eyes roamed each book and I was shocked to see the type of material she read. She had everything from The Coldest Winter Ever to Twilight.

"What you know about the 48 Laws of Power?" I asked, pulling the book from the shelf. Just like any other nigga, I read the book while I was locked up in Rikers Island serving an eight-year bid.

"'When you are trying to impress people with words, the more you say, the more common you appear, and the less in control. Always say less than necessary.'" She looked at me and smiled. "I read that book when I was 14. My father brought it home one day and made sure I read it. Most of these books belong to him or my mother. I just kept them along with their other important things. I nodded, impressed. Queen was fine as fuck, could shoot a gun, had some good ass pussy and could read; yeah, I was in love.

"I'm 'bout to go lay down. You gone cook a nigga somthing to eat? I need some real food." I slapped her on the ass.

"I can whip you up something," she said and walked over to the kitchen. I watched her open the fridge and began pulling things out. "How does a stuffed potato with shrimp and crab meat sound?" she asked.

"Good, if you know what you doing." I smirked.

"Boy, I do my shit." She playfully rolled her eyes.

"We gone see," I told her then clutched my crutch and leapt into her bedroom.

When I walked in, I stopped to look around her bedroom. Just as the living room, her shit was extra clean, all white minus the satin gold blanket on her bed. Her headboard and matching dresser was white and she had a few decorative trinkets that matched the blanket. Noticing a few pictures, I walked over to her dresser and picked up the first picture. It was a picture of Queen with a white puppy. She appeared to be about nine or ten and I could tell from the two ponytails she wore that hung long. Sitting the picture down, I picked up the next picture and studied it. I stared at the picture for so long I never noticed Queen standing behind me.

"You want some..." she went to say but stopped mid-sentence. "My mom and dad." She looked at me then at the picture. For a brief moment, I remained silent then I looked over at her.

"You look just like yo moms." I sat the picture back down and took a seat on the bed.

"Everybody says that. Lots of people say I look like my father too."

"Yeah, you do. Aye where the remote at? You got Netflix? I wanna check out that movie I've been hearing about. With the kids that the DA forced a case on."

"When They See Us."

"Yeah, that."

"I watched it, finally. It was pretty good."

"Yeah, I keep hearing."

"It's four hours long, you staying that long?"

"Why, you want me to leave?"

"No," she said and walked over to me. She placed her hands on my knees and bent down to kiss me.

"Good, 'cause I ain't never leaving." I smirked and pulled a pillow from the head of the bed. She walked out of the room and I grabbed the remote. I knew I wouldnt make it through the entire four hours because the meds they had me on was strong as fuck. But a nigga was gonna at least try to hang in there until Queen was done cooking.

Twenty

Sincere

After a few days of cuddling with Queen, watching movies and fucking her until she needed a new hair do, I was up at 5:30 in the morning on a cold mission. Shit needed to be handled that had to do with me being shot. Yesterday, Cordell's people reached out to me on some peace shit. The first thing they mentioned was they didn't have shit to do with me getting shot. After that call, I began to place the pieces together and I knew exactly who it was. One phone call and I got the exact details I needed so it was time to roll out.

Before I turned to leave, I looked at Queen to make sure she was still asleep. When I heard the light snores that escaped her mouth I left her crib and hopped into my whip. I sent her a text that I would be back later, started my engine and headed for my prey. With the pedal to the metal I had arrived in no time. I parked my whip and pulled my phone out to make a call.

"Hello?"

"I'm outside," I spoke into the phone and then disconnected it. Moments later, the gate opened so I climbed out to walk inside. I was gonna leave my whip outside the gate just in case I needed to make a break for it. I was still slightly limping but right now I felt like The Incredible Hulk. I was so eager I didn't even think about the pain. As a matter of fact, I had to be feeling better than I thought because I began to jog up the driveway. When I made it to the door, it was slightly ajar so I slid inside. The entire home was quiet so I made sure to creep across the marble floor discreetly. I pulled my strap from my waistband and held it on my side. Knowing exactly what door I was heading into, I slid right up on it and pushed it open.

"Wake up, old man. Your death date has finally come." I struck him across the head with the butt of my gun. He began to stir in his sleep and when he finally realized what was going on, he shot up and stared down my cold eyes.

"Si...Sinn...shit!" he stuttered nervously.

"Surprised to see me?" I asked tauntingly. "You might as well make this easy on both of us, Frank. You know the routine, get up and lay flat on your stomach." Franko looked at me then slightly shook his head. He wore a drafted look because he knew his final days had come. Franko knew me and he knew me well. He knew when I showed up it meant death. I wasn't the type of nigga to play, which is why we didn't fuck with each any longer.

Before I became a dopeboy, I used to do hits for this nigga. He had me running around on some wild shit killing anything he demanded. I was a young nigga out here starving and the money he paid was well worth every kill. Shit, I would kill a nigga for crumbs so I might as well got paid for it. As I got older I realized I made enough money to leave that shit alone but Franko had other plans for me. He always told me that death was the only way out, but he had me all the way fucked up. I was having shoot-outs everytime my feet hit the pavement. I used lots of my bread to cop more guns because I knew what it was going up after a nigga like Franko. One by one, I took out every muthafucka he sent my way and even nearly took his life. The only reason I didn't was because he waved his white flag and gave me a quarter of a million and his words exactly were "you won."

I took the bread and left the nigga alone. I didn't have any more problems out of him up until the day I went to jail. When I stopped working for Franko, I copped me some dope and went headfirst into that field. I built me a cold ass team of niggas and before I knew it, we had taken over the entire city. Out of nowhere, one day, I was pulled over by the police with a bird in my trunk. The shit was crazy because they went straight to my stash. At first I thought it was a nigga on my team ratting me out but nah, the entire time it was the bitch ass nigga, Franko.

Because I didn't have any priors I was given eight years. Taking my time like a G, I went to give the system seven years off the eight and possibly six on good behavior. On one particular visit, I was called into the chapel by Mayor Jones. He sat me down and explained to me that Franko was the one that had set me up. The only reason I didn't come right away to kill the nigga was because he had the police in his pocket. However, the day had finally come just as I expected. And just like I knew he awaited my arrival because his face didn't show one sign of fear.

"May I?" he asked, holding up a Cuban cigar. I didn't bother replying so he took it upon himself to grab his lighter and set fire to it. After taking a few pulls, he finally looked over at me.

"You know she doesn't want you," he said and took a drag from his cigar. "She's in love with the dead guy." He never once looked at me. I knew instantly he was referring to Queen and it was something about the sound in his voice that made me clench my jaw. "You know, Sincere, I actually used to like you. I respected your hand. You know you reminded me a lot of myself when I was your age. Hungry, eager and determined." He took another hit and turned to finally make eye contact with me. "Remember this: in this game, everyone dies. When you stepped into my world, you sold your soul. Remember what I told you a long time ago? The only way out is death," he chuckled. My finger was on my trigger, itching to blow this nigga away.

"You kill me, somebody kills you," he said and turned his head.

"Fuck you." I seethed and pulled the trigger. I didn't even wait for him to lie down. I blew his shit back from a clean side shot. His body sat still for a few moments before it fell to the side lifeless. His brain had splattered all over his bedding, leaving chunks on his pillow. I watched him for a few more seconds before I turned to leave.

As I walked out, I took the long hallway right to the front door. Just as I neared the foyer, the smell of cigarette smoke made me look over. I knew exactly who it was. Jizzle and I locked eyes as she blew the smoke from her mouth. That same cold glare that she wore years ago was etched on her face. I swear this lady was something else. I couldn't say I didn't blame her because she knew the real Franko and the real Franko wasn't shit. Jizzle was a savage in my book and after she had just set this up for me, I really respected her.

Really, this was a long time favor she owed me since she paid me to kill Natalie, Franko's first wife. Nodding my head once, Jizzle spoke to me without saying a word. She blew that last cloud of smoke before smashing the cigarette into the ashtray. With nothing else left to say, I headed out the door and to my car. I was contemplating going back to Queen's but instead, I headed home. I needed to find my wife and see where her head was at.

Twenty One

Queen

Rubbing my hand across the name that read Marcellus Jackson, a lone tear slid from my face. I placed the flowers onto his headstone and fell into a daze. I closed my eyes and began to have those same visions of him walking in the yard with the food. That illusion was supposed to be our life but it never happened. I began to think about what Franko said and the more I relished on it, the more dismal I became. Cellus was my life. After my parents were murdered he made me feel whole again. He not only supported my broken heart but he was truly my rock.

"I met someone." I looked down at his gravesite. The breeze that rubbed across my cheek made me look into the sky and fall into a daze. "I really like him." I continued to speak as the sun kissed my cheeks. "I don't know about the white picket fence yet but he's a cool guy, Cellus." I looked down and another tear slid down my face. "I love you, Cellus. I'll never forget you no matter what. Things with this guy are confusing but I think I wanna give him a chance."

I kissed my finger and placed it on his headstone. I stood to my feet and before walking off, an aircraft came flying through the sky. There were four planes that I could see perfectly clear. When they began to circle the cemetery, I finally realized why. Every 4th, 14th and 24th of the month, they would do laps in remembrance of my parents, which made me think about the fact that I had forgotten their death anniversary. Every year they held these memorials but it's not like I ever attended. I didn't bother with my parents' life and I damn sure didn't trust not a soul in the CIA. Everyone on the force was guilty in my eyes so I made sure to keep my distance.

After watching the planes fly away, I crossed my hand over my chest into a cross then kissed it into Heaven. Letting out a soft sigh, I headed to my car and climbed in. Just as I fell into my seat, my phone rang, causing me to look down. *Jizzle?* I thought, wondering why was she calling me. I knew it had to be important because she never called.

"Hey, Jizzle."

"Oh my God, Queen," she cried into the phone.

"Is everything okay?"

"No. Franko was found dead in our home last night." My mouth fell open and my heart sank. Right now Franko wasn't on my best person list, but hearing he had been killed left me a bit dismal. The way Franko moved in these streets there was no telling who could have been behind it.

"Break in," she added, grabbing my attention.

"I'm so sorry, Jizz. I'll be by to see you."

"Okay," she continued to weep and then disconnected the line.

"Queen, you gotta toughen up. Remember two rules in this house. No bitches allowed, and love doesn't exist. I'm gonna take you and make you into the most Treacherous woman in the world."

"And how are you gonna do that?"

"Oh trust me, my child, you'll see soon. Very very soon." He nodded his head. *"Have you ever shot a gun?"* he asked, knowing damn well I was a young and timid girl. I mean I visit the projects often but I didn't indulge in the usual violent activities.

"No," I shook my head sadly. I was still gloomy because of my par-

ents' deaths.

"*Well, you're gonna learn today.*"

The sound of my phone ringing again brought me from my short daze. When I looked at the screen it was Sincere. He had left yesterday and I hadn't seen him nor heard from him since. Something in my gut told me he had gone home to rekindle with his wife so I was in my feelings. Therefore, I didn't bother answering, instead, I started my engine and headed home.

Pulling up to my home, I drove into the underground parking and grabbed my Blue Ribbon bag and headed upstairs. Just as I turned the corner, Sin was walking down the hall as if he had just come from my door.

"Hey." I greeted him and stuck my key into the door. He followed me inside and took a seat on the sofa. I paid close attention to the way he was walking and he appeared to be doing much better. I also noticed he was using his crutch but when he took a seat he slightly flinched. I headed into the kitchen to grab the hot sauce and then walked back into the room to join him on the sofa.

"Where you been and why you ain't been answering my calls?"

"Cemetery and I have a lot of things on my mind."

"Things like what?" he asked, reaching over to grab a piece of chicken from my tray.

"I missed my parents' memorial," I told him so he could kill the subject.

"Damn," he said and looked at me. "Is that who you went to see?"

"No. I went to see Cellus." I replied, pulling a French fry from the bag.

"Cellus?" he repeated his name and then fell silent. I didn't bother replying. "Yo ex?"

"If that's what you wanna call him."

"So that's why you ain't answer?" he began shaking his head.

"So now I gotta compete with a dead nigga?" he asked, catching me off guard. I turned to look at him like he had lost his damn mind.

"Excuse me?" I shot and sat my food down on the table. I knew where this conversation was going and right now food was the last thing on my mind.

"You heard what the fuck I said, ma. You supposed to be my bitch but going to vist this nigga. Nah, I don't give a fuck about the history shit y'all had. You belong to me now so all your memories of this nigga need to cease."

"First off, nigga, I ain't yo bitch. Second, you have your fucking nerves after you disappeard on me. Now what I do with Cellus is none of your fucking business. Your business is at home with your fucking wife."

"Thanks to you, I ain't got no wife." He jumped to his feet. He walked towards the door and that shit pissed me off more. I hated when someone called them self dismissing me. I stood up and stormed over to the door behind him. When he turned the knob to open it, I expected for him to turn around and apologize but instead, he walked out and never looked back.

I furiously slammed the door behind him and plopped down on the sofa. I crossed my arms over one another and began to think about Franko's word. In a sense he made perfectly good sense. Love was just a distraction and the way Sin had me feeling I was ready go the fuck off. I looked at my phone that sat on the table and I wanted so badly to give him a piece of my mind. How dare he speak on something that was before him. Cellus was long gone so him feeling like he would have to compete with a man that was deceased was the stupidest shit I've heard in my life. Just thinking about it, made me shake my head. Instead of calling him, I got up and headed into my room. I was gonna go see Jizzle so I could take my mind off the situation.

When I stepped foot into Franko's home, I didn't get that normal warm feeling I often got. Instead there was a cold and erie feeling that swept through my body causing me to halt for a brief moment. When one of the guards noticed me he greeted me and informed me that Jizzle was inside of Franko's study. Heading up the long stairs, I headed to the door and then lightly knocked. Instead of waiting for a response, I pushed it open and stepped inside. Jizzle was sitting behind the desk in tune with whatever she was watching on the computer. She was so into it, she didn't move her eyes from the screen to look up at me. The sound of a woman moaning made me wonder what she was watching so I stepped closer to her desk to get a peek.

"Did you know about this?" she asked without looking over. I didn't bother to reply, instead I focused on the screen and watched Nelly fuck the life out of Franko.

"Nothing that man does surprises me." I sighed and took a seat. I didn't want to see it anymore.

"The bitch is dead," Jizzle spoke with venom. I didn't know if she meant she killed her already or was she gonna kill her but either way I knew she was serious.

"He wanted a gold casket with a white and gold suit. I found it strange for a man to love lillies but those were his requests," she paused briefly and then continued. "You know when I first met Franko I thought he was the most handsome man on earth. His demeanor and striking suit attracted me to him. The way he smoked a cigar intrigued me. As time went by, I began to realize that a person's exterior is the total opposite from his interior. He seemed like the perfect man on the outside but he was a damn devil. I was in love with a devil." She shook her head and looked back over to the computer. "I guess it's true, you lose 'em how you get 'em." She turned to look at me. "How's Sincere?" she asked as if she knew something.

"He's...um..." I tried to shy away from the question. However, it puzzled me to know how she knew Sin. "How do you know, Sincere?"

"Chile, Sincere's been around the family for years. He actually worked for us." She turned to look at me. "And by the look on your face, I take it you didn't know?" I shook my head no because I had no idea. Of course I never mentioned Franko to Sin and because Franko had plenty of hidden agendas, he never mentioned why he wanted Sin dead.

"Like I said, nothing Franko does seems to amaze me." I stood to my feet. "What day and time is the service?"

"Thursday, all white, nine sharp," she said and turned towards the computer. I could tell that she had been sitting in this same spot for hours watching Franko and Nelly's tapes. I couldn't understand for the life of me why she would want to tourture herself.

"I'll see you real soon," I replied and headed out the door. I knew that sooner or later Jizzle and I would have a serious talk. I had questions and she had answers. Just by her demeanor and questions, I knew she knew more than she mentioned. Not only that, but it was something about the look in her eyes at the mention of Sincere that wasn't adding up.

Twenty Two

Sincere

What type of games is being played, how's it going down?
It's on till it's gone, then I got to know now
Is you wit' me or what, wake up try to get me a nut
'Cause hunnies give me the butt, what?

As I drove towards the cementary to Franko's burial, a nigga's mind was in overdrive. I took in the lyrics to DMX's How It's Going Down and Queen crossed my mind. It had been over a week since the last time I saw her and every day she was on my mind heavy. I thought about the day I stormed out her crib and the argument we had. I really didn't mean to offend her but the shit Franko had said weighed heavy on me. She's in love with the dead guy played over and over in my mind so when she mentioned she went to the cemetery to visit his grave, I lost it. After that day, it was evident that I had fallen in love with her no matter how hard I tried to deny it.

However, I wasn't about to compete with a dead nigga and I meant it. I know it sounded selfish because I still had Helen who was actually sitting in my passenger seat smacking her lips. I guess she knew that I was thinking about Queen while listening to this song. Since the night I had killed Franko, Helen came back home so we could talk. We talked, we fucked and she ended up coming back home. It's like the more time I spent with her I realized I wasn't happy and I knew it had to do with Queen. I guess Helen sensed it because she told me everything about me felt different.

When I woke up this morning and began to get dressed for Franko's funeral, she badgered me about going to see Queen and that shit got on my last nerve. And this was the reason I brought her along right now so she could shut the fuck up. However, I made up my mind that once this service was done, I was gonna drop her off and go holla at Queen. A part of me didn't even wanna attend because really it was fuck Franko. But Jizzle called me two days ago and asked if I could come. She also mentioned she wanted me to meet someone. The way she sounded was as if it was important and knowing the life Jizzle lived, I knew it had to be.

Pulling up to the service, I had a clear view of everyone forming a circle around Franko's casket. Out of respect, I turned down my music and headed up the slight hill so I could park. I motioned for Helen to get out and she slid her frames down on her face and then stepped out the whip. We made our way towards the family and the minute we stepped amongst the crowd Queen and I locked eyes. Her eyes shifted from me to Helen and then she quickly turned her head to focus on the service. Her eyes were covered in a pair of oversized Chanel frames but I could feel her stealing glances in my direction. I focused on Jizzle who sat in the front row and cried like she was hurt. She was putting on a Grammy performance with the way she was sobbing. If I didn't know any better, I'd feel bad for her but the shit was all an act. Scanning the crowd, I watched all the men in their expensive suits and a few guards that I had known from fucking with Franko. When I turned to face the pastor, my eyes fell onto Queen again. I couldn't help it.

"Why would you bring me here knowing she was here?" Helen spoke just above a whisper.

"Not here," I told her because I didn't have time to entertain her jealousy.

My mind began to roam and I thought about the picture on Queen's dresser. It was her parents and it all began to make sense. All I could do was shake my head because Franko really wasn't shit. And this was another reason I had been keeping my distance because of guilt. I shook my head and then turned just in time to catch a glimpse of the doves that had been released into the sky. Shortly after they flew away, the crowd began to disperse. Queen shot me one last look and then headed over to Jizzle's side. She bent down and whispered into her ear, and rubbed her back for comfort. The entire time I watched her and didn't care that Helen was on the side of me.

"Excuse me," I told Helen and walked over to Jizzle. Jizzle was now standing up and she appeared to feel a lot better. *This woman really ain't shit like her dead ass husband,* I thought, shaking my head. Before I could make it to Queen, she had been pulled away by some nigga who wore a white suit like the rest of the pallbearers.

"Sincere, thank you for coming." Jizzle reached out for a hug. "Maxwell, please come meet Sin," she called out to a man who stood nearby. He walked over to me and shook my hand. "We will have a further meeting after today but Sin I want you next in command. I think you're fit to take over what Franko has left behind."

"Wow, I didn't expect that. But real shit, Jizzle, I don't know about that. A nigga been left that shit alone." I looked off into the air. I had enough bloody money and plenty of bodies under my belt and I was still breathing and not in a jail cell. Therefore, I was beginning to feel like I needed to get out before it was too late. And that's what I had been contemplating on these last few days.

"Is it because you're in love?" she asked with her eyes trained on Queen. I looked ahead in Queen's direction and she was still smiling in ol' boy's face. All the smiling and giggling she was doing had a nigga slightly jealous.

"Do you believe in karma?" Jizzle asked as we both continued to look in Queen's direction.

"Nah," was my only response.

"Well, believe it, it's true. I'll be seeing you around," she said and patted me on the back. I stood frozen in a daze because of her last words. I knew what she meant because Jizzle knew about the demise I had caused. However, I prayed the shit didn't bite me in the ass and karma came back to suck my dick.

As bad as I didn't want to come to the after service, I was curious to see if Queen would attend. I dropped Helen off at home so this was my chance to get baby back in my good graces. I knew she was gonna trip off me being back with Helen but I was gonna assure her that if she gave me the chance I would shake Helen for sure.

When I pulled up to Franko and Jizzle's crib, the house brought back so many memories. Some good, some bad but most of all the shit left wild memories. There was a time Franko and I were cool. Cool enough that I would come over and indulge in their often thrown festivities. I was cool with Jizzle and Franko's pops who had actually passed him his throne. Right now the yard was full of his family and friends who I was sure got their hands dirty. Everybody Franko associated with indulged in some type of illegal activities.

I walked into the yard and began to scan the crowd for Jizzle. When I didn't see her, I headed over to the bar and placed an order for a bottle. Because I didn't trust these muthafuckas, I was gonna get the entire bottle and make sure my shit was properly sealed. After getting my drink, I headed over to talk to Maxwell, one of Franko's new hitmans. Just as I was nearing him, I spotted Queen over by the pool talking to the same guy she was talking to at the cemetery. Again a jealousy shot through my body as I watched her smiling all in the niggas face. She had a cup in her hand and I could tell she was a bit tipsy. Instead of stopping to holla at Maxwell, I walked up on Queen.

"Can I holla at you for a minute, Queen?" I asked in my most polite voice. She looked over and then turned her head to face ol' boy. I chuckled to myself because I was tryna keep from spazzing out. "Bring yo muthafucking ass here," I said and snatched her by the arm. She had me all the way fucked up.

"Why the fuck...?"

"Man, because you ignoring a nigga like I'm just some bitch ass nigga. Queen, you think I give a fuck about any of these people? I'll beat yo ass in here."

"Nigga, you wouldnt stand a chance." Her drunk ass smiled and rolled her neck.

"Try me. I'll kung fu kick yo ass so hard, girl," I told her and she slightly chuckled.

"What do you want, Sincere?"

"You," I replied and looked her in the eyes. Her big pretty eyes looked up at me and then she dropped her head to the ground. I hated when she did this because she was trying to break our eye contact. "Q Bee, look at me," I demanded. When she looked back up, I began pouring my heart out to her. "It ain't what you think. For real. Yes, I ended up back with Helen but my heart not there. I'm in love with you and all I need is you to tell me you wanna give us a chance. I know this shit is sudden but I promise I won't hurt you. I don't know why, but it's like I found my soulmate in you and this where I wanna be. Just give us a chance." I held her hand in mine as I looked her in the eyes. She never took her eyes off me but she did blink a few times to blink her tears away. She squeezed my hand and her face sank with sorrow.

"For many years, I was supposed to believe that love didn't exist. It's like I lost a passion for love and the whole ideal of having a family and someone that may have been truly in my corner. I'm willing to take a chance with you, Sin, but I'm scared of being let down. So many people in my life have let me down that it put me in this shell. I hate that I've come between you and your wife but I can't help how I feel. Everyday I've thought of you and even sometimes cried." When she said that, my heart dropped.

"I'm sorry, ma," I spoke penitently as I matched her stare.

"I want the white picket fence, love." She looked at me as if I would object. "I wanna play in the sun with my children, Sin. Do you like Chinese food?" she asked out of nowhere. It was something about the sparkle in her eyes when she spoke of the picket fence and playing in the sun. The whole thought of having children made a nigga smile inside. I wanted kids so badly but that was something Helen couldn't give me.

"Four kids," I told her and she quickly looked at me.

"Three." She smirked, making me chuckle.

"Girl, you gone give me about five. Bring yo ass here," I told her and pulled her in for a kiss. For a split second, I forgot where we were. Right now, I didn't care. I was happy to have my baby back and after this, I was gonna make her not only love a nigga, but forget about her tainted past. Keep shit real, because of my past and the shit I've done, I owed her that much.

Twenty Three

John

After watching Queen and who I assumed was her boyfriend for nearly an hour, I started my engine to proceed home. The pain I felt in my heart made me wanna run my car into the Atlantic Ocean. Just seeing her, hugging and kissing him, pained me. When he threw her over his shoulder and she began giggling, it killed me more. I knew now this was the reason Queen had basically forgotten about me. She had been so distant she left me heartbroken. I drove myself crazy, researching everything about her past life. I had found out everything from her real name to her parents' murder. What I didn't understand was, what type of life was she into because she had been so secretive. She even had me believing her name was really Queen when in fact, it was Reina Clarke. I couldn't understand for the life me why would someone lie unless they had something to hide.

Ring...

"Hello, hello..." I spoke into the phone eagerly.

"Hey, John, just returning your call."

"Scott, thanks, man. Sorry to bother you but I need a huge favor."

"If I could help, I'm here," he chuckled into the phone.

"Do you remember the Clarke case? Agents murdered in their home."

"How can I forget? King was a good buddy of mine."

"I see. Well, their daughter is a great friend of mines and I was helping her do a bit of research about their murder," I lied.

"Reina?"

"Yes, Reina Clarke."

"How is she doing? You know since I've moved I haven't heard from her. Her parents left something for her that I still have but I haven't been able to contact her."

"She's doing great. I'm actually on my way over to her home." Again, I lied.

"Well, I'm all the way in Kentucky, if you can come down I'll give you the report and the letter I have. It's still sealed."

"Uh, sure. I'll come now." Again, he began to chuckle. I was gonna take the long flight and for Queen it was worth it. He began giving me the information I needed and advised us to meet at the airport. After thanking him, I hung up the phone and headed home so I could make up a lie to give to my wife. I knew when I got a hold of the information he had I could use this to get Queen back.

Queen

"I love you, Sincere! Oooh, shit! I love you, babe," I cried out in ecstasy as Sin blew my back out. He had my legs spread open as the heel of my feet rested into the palm of his hands. He was hitting me with nice long strokes and every so many minutes he would speed up his pace. The way he was controlling my body had me not only submissive but captive. It's like he held my love box as a prisoner and he was the only person to visit. I don't know what this man had done to me but he had taken over my soul. Don't get me wrong, it wasn't just his enthralling sex, it was the chemistry between us that made everythig much more intense.

"Baby, I gotta..."

"Man, you gotta throw up again?" He stopped to look at me. Without replying, I jumped to my feet and ran full speed into the restroom. *Lord, make it stop,* I thought as I stood to my feet and headed over to the washbowl to brush my teeth for the third time today.

"Man, yo ass need to go to the doctor. I think a nigga done shot one in you," Sin said, standing in the doorway.

"Sin, I'm not pregnant. It was that damn liquor and then yo ass rocking me in the bed. I'm fine."

"Aight, well, if yo ass still like this by Monday we going."

"Okay," I agreed so he could leave it alone. I knew I wasn't pregnant because I had a period last month and wasn't due again until the 27th. I knew my body. It was the liquor and Sin wasn't making it any better by rocking the got damn boat.

"I hope you is pregnant." He smiled from the bed. He was

under the cover looking like he had been drained out. We had been fucking for hours and he had already nutted twice. Earlier today we went to an Italian restaurant and like always Sin ordered a bottle of champagne. By the time we were done, we went through three bottles and almost couldn't drive home. The moment we walked into the door, he stripped me from my clothing and we had been at it since. We fucked from the living room to the kitchen into the bedroom.

"Why you smiling?" I asked because out of nowhere a huge grin crept up on his face.

"Just thinking."

"'Bout?"

"You and the possibility of you giving me my first seed."

"And what if I'm not pregnant?"

"Shit, Ima keep going until you are. Come here, baby, lay down." He patted the side next to him. The minute I climbed into bed he yawned and I could tell he was tired.

"Baby, go to sleep." I cuddled underneath him and began rubbing my hands through his locks.

"I love you," he spoke, half asleep.

"I love you more," I whispered soothingly into his ear. The music softly played in the background and the flicker from the single candle made our shadows dance off the wall. I continued to rub Sin's locs and kissed him a few times. I couldn't help but smile thinking about how magical things were over the last few weeks. Sin had done everything in his power to win me over and I'd be lying if I said it didn't work. He hadn't been back home and each time Helen called him he wouldn't bother to answer. He had his guards keep watch of his home and he even went to buy clothing so he wouldn't have to go.

Everyday was a different adventure. We had been out to eat, sailing on his yacht and to my surprise he agreed to snorkel with me. A few days we stayed inside and watched movies cuddled up. The only time he left was to go check on his money and each time he invited me for the ride. Just being with Sin had me feeling whole. I haven't felt this complete in my life and I feel like I

BARBIE SCOTT

deserved it. He made me realize that love did, in fact, exist and I was happy I took the chance. *Damn,* I cursed myself because I could hear my phone ringing from the living room. This was the third time it had rang and I did my best to ignore it. Letting out an aggravated sigh, I slid from under Sin and headed into the living room to power it off.

Looking at my screen, the number wasn't stored. This was odd because no one ever called me. No one had my number but a few people that I didn't deal with daily. Franko was dead and Sin was asleep in my bed. Curiosity began to get the best of me, and for some odd reason, I thought it may be Helen.

"Hello?" I answered unsurely.

"Queen, I need you to listen to me," the voice spoke into the phone. I pulled the phone away from my ear puzzled as to whom the caller was.

"How did you get my number?" I asked with my guard up.

"Right now that doesn't matter. I really n...."

"I can't talk right now, John. I'm busy so I'll..."

"Queen, would you happen to have a 48 Laws of Power book?"

"Uhh? Yes, but why are you asking me this?" I looked behind me to make sure Sin was still asleep. I don't know how John had gotten my number but I was beginning to feel creeped out. John didn't know anything about me except my name was Queen, which wasn't really my name. Not even Sin knew my real name and I planned on keeping it that way. Queen was not only my alias because of my line of work, I had the name so I could avoid the agents and anyone else associated with my old life.

"Nooo, please! Listen to me, Queen. Look inside the book. There's a letter or something there your parents left you."

"John, look, I advise..." Again, he cut me off.

"Queen, look in the got damn book! King and Lauren left a letter the day they were murdered." Hearing him mention my parents made me freeze up. I turned to look at the bookshelf and my eyes fell onto the 48 Laws of Power novel. I slowly crept over to the shelf and my hands slightly shook nervously. When I

124

grabbed the book, I began flipping through the pages.

"Page 48," John spoke eagerly. I went to page 48 and true enough, there was a letter and a picture. I flipped the picture over and I became stunned. It was a picture of Sincere standing outdoors on his phone. I began to read the letter and the more I read, the more my heart sank.

Reina,

If you received this letter more than likely your father and I are dead. We can't write long because our killer is outside. This is the picture of the man that's gonna take our lives, and he was hired by Franko. Whatever you do, just go far away from him. Call this number and Alana will have some money for you. Please, my child, leave New York and figure things out.

Love you, Mom & Dad

As I read the letter, tears poured from my eyes. I looked over the picture of Sincere and my heart broke into a million pieces. *He killed my parents*, I thought as my hands shook harder. I kept telling myself this had to be a joke but everything had begun to make sense. The day Sin saw the picture of my parents, he had this weird look on his face. Not only that but, him being associated with Franko, and now knowing Franko's disloyalty, I knew this was possible.

Trust me, if you knew the real about Sincere, you'd forget all about him.

Franko's words began to play in my mind. It was something about the look in his eyes when he said those words that didn't sit well with me but I ignored it.

"Queen, you okay?" I jumped to the sound of Sincere's voice.

"I'm...uh...I'm okay," I replied and quickly closed the book. I slid it back onto the shelf along with my phone because I heard John call out to me.

"You sure you good, ma?" he asked, stepping closer to me. This time my entire body began to tremble and I prayed he didn't get near me.

"Yes. Let's go lay back down." I headed into the room and he followed closely behind.

"You not thinking 'bout that nigga, is you?" he asked, upset.

"Sin, I told you I'm over that." I let out a sigh. "Why would I think about him when I have you right here." I pulled him down onto the bed and began kissing him. "Ready for round four?" I seductively whispered into his ear.

"You know I'm always ready." He flipped me over so I could straddle him. I slightly lifted up so he could slide inside of me and I moaned louder with every inch that filled my tunnel. I began to slowly ride him and bent down to kiss him passionately. Suddenly tears began to pour from my eyes but I didn't stop grinding my hips.

"I love you, Sincere," my heart cried out to him. I was in love with this man.

I slid my hand to the head of my bed and began gripping the sheets. Sin began to kiss me on the neck and then he pulled my head down forcefully to look me in the eyes.

"I love you, ma." His words sounded so sincere he made my tears pour at a rapid speed.

"Sin I love you too, but love don't exist." I slid my hand from the edge, and without warning, I sliced him across the neck from one ear to the other.

His eyes shot open wide because it still hadn't registered. His blood began to seep from his neck and clutched it with both hands. He looked at his hands and when he noticed blood, he looked over at me but it was too late. His body slumped back slowly and he died right here in my bed. Not being able to stop the tears, I reached down to place a sensual kiss on Sin's lips. At this very moment, my life began to flash before my eyes. And I began to realize that love really didn't exist in my world.

The Epilogue

Three years later...

"One, two, three! You're it!" I ran full speed around to the side of my home. When I looked back, Sin'Marie was hot on my heels. Her two pigtails danced with each step and the huge smile plastered on her face made me stop to laugh.

"Got you!" my baby girl giggled and she fell into my arms. I playfully fell into the grass and pulled her on top of me to tickle her.

"Mommy, stooop...ughhhh, stop." She laughed so hard she almost peed her pants.

"Come on, Sin, let's go eat." I pulled her by the arms so she could stand to her feet. Moments later, Max, our puppy, ran into the yard so I closed the white picket fence behind him.

"What are we eating?" Sin asked, holding my hands up the stairs.

"Chinese."

"Yaaay! I love Chinese, Mommy!" she yelled excitedly and it made me smile.

Those visions I often had, had come true but it didn't pan out how I imagined. I only had one child but I did get my white picket fence. Instead of the love of my life bringing me Chinese food, Sin'Marie and I ate together. Everytime I looked at her, she looked so much like Sincere I'd often wanna cry. However, I finally realized *Love Did Exist* when God blessed me with my daughter. It wasn't that exact vision but this was the semblance of an illusion and I was finally happy. It was just me and Sin'Marie and this was how it would be forever. John came by to see us but we haven't been intimate. I was done with married men; however, we would always remain friends.

The End...

Visit My Website
http://authorbarbiescott.com/?v=7516fd43adaa

Barbie Scott Book Trap (Book Club) click below to see
character visuals, enter contests and have literary fun with polls.
https://www.facebook.com/groups/1624522544463985/

Like My Page On Facebook
https://www.facebook.com/
AuthorBarbieScott/?modal=composer

Instagram:
https://www.instagram.com/authorbarbiescott/?hl=en

CPSIA information can be obtained
at www.ICGtesting.com
Printed in the USA
LVHW020114150820
663222LV00013B/1079

9 798646 713590